I0536003

A.B.Normal
Publishing and Media Group
Anything but normal.

A.B.Normal Publishing and Media Group

PO Box 31311

Knoxville, TN 37930

www.abnormalpublishing.com

Publisher's note: The story, all names, characters, and incidents portrayed in this production are fictitious. No identification with actual persons (living or deceased), places, buildings, and products is intended or should be inferred.

Hardback ISBN: 978-1-7350597-2-3

Paperback ISBN: 978-1-7350597-4-7

eBook ISBN: 978-1-7350597-3-0

Library of Congress Control Number: 2025911907

Edited by Rachel Small. Original Cover/Title Art by Jake Clark. Updated art by Alan B. N. Penman. Original story The Chronicles of Bob: The Chronic Suicidal by Robert J. McCartney.

First Print, 2025. Published in Knoxville, TN.

CONTENTS

To my wife and kids.

To my friends and family: thanks for all your support and encouraging words.

For the friends and family that I have lost.

Having a mental illness is difficult. Don't let it consume you, your life, your dreams, your family, and your friends. Fight back against the darkness. For all those who think they're alone, who wander alone. You are not alone. For those who have thought about suicide, and for those who have. For all those lost and forgotten. Don't let it be a taboo—don't let it be swept under the rug that society has created. Don't be ashamed to ask for help. Rise, and together, we can help each other. The strength we desire and need to carryon is inside of us. We don't have to carry this burden alone. — RJM

> "Not all those who wander are lost."
> J. R. R. Tolkien

> "You're only given a little spark of madness. You mustn't lose it."
> Robin Williams

> "Be anything but normal."
> Robert J. McCartney

Read Book Two in the Willborne Saga *Requiem for Lilith*,
available along with other titles.

Visit www.abnormalpublishing.com for free stories,
information, and more.

Scan this QR code for
Requiem for Lilith

Read Book Two in the Willborne Saga *Lilah's Guide to Hoyle*, available along with other titles.

Visit www.abnormalpublishing.com for free stories, information, and more.

Scan this QR code for
Lilah's Guide to Hoyle

Trigger Warning/Disclaimer
(Because Apparently We Need One):

Look, before you dive in, let's get this out of the way. This book deals with some heavy shit: suicide, self-harm, substance abuse, drugs, violence, and a whole list of things you really shouldn't try at home—or anywhere, for that matter.

Honestly, I didn't think I'd need to spell that out, but hey, here we are. It's 2025. Back when the other Bob wrote this in 2017, the world was already sideways. Now? It's doing cartwheels in a dumpster fire.

So yeah. This is your warning. A disclaimer. A flashing neon sign that says, "Turn back if you're easily rattled or expecting sunshine and life lessons."

This isn't that kind of ride.
This is Bob. And Bob's not
alright.

You were warned.

With love,
Bob ☺

WHAT IS THE DEFINITION?

CHRONIC SUICIDAL:

*Chron·ic sui·cid·al /□krä-nik \ □sü-ə-□sī-dɒl *
Adjective

1. A person who suffers from chronic suicidal ideation and carries out suicide multiple times.

2. An impulsive and compulsive individual with the desire to kill themselves regularly.

3. One who attempts or commits suicide a lot, i.e., Bob, the Chronic Suicidal.

4. A suicidal individual who kills himself repetitively due to the want or need or "itch."

MY ADDITION—A person who "kills" themselves to process trauma, heartache, existential dread, and the crushing absurdity of life, not to escape it, but to *understand* it.

To reclaim power. To evolve.

It is not an end. It's a reckoning. A ritual. A response.

We are not bound to definitions or labels. So, break the rules. Break the mold. Break the cycle.

Keep. Moving. Forward.

— Bob

PREFACE

I didn't write this to be funny.

Well, okay, I did. But not just for laughs.

This started as an outlet. A way to escape my thoughts. Reality. The weight. The darkness. I was never going to actually hurt anyone—not myself, not others—but damn if I didn't feel the pull.

I'm a survivor on a lot of levels—suicide, abuse, neglect. Some folks would contest that, swear I had "the good life," and try to slap a fresh coat of nostalgia on my trauma like it's going to cover the bloodstains. But I know better. And I know I'm not alone.

So, I came up with a plan. I'd kill myself—again and again—on the page.

Bob was born out of that. He dies, so I don't have to. He suffers, and through him, I process.

At first, it was an experiment. Then it became a blog. Then, something more.

Bob's story became a way to understand myself. To face death in a thousand ways and still find a reason to return. To give others still struggling *a shot*. A flicker of "Hey, maybe I'm not the only one."

It's dark. It's absurd. It's angry. It's also mine. I fight back with a black pen and a darker sense of humor. And in turn, it's yours. Ours.

So if you're out there—if you're hurting—just know this wasn't written to glorify anything. It was written to *survive*.

And with that . . . without further ado . . .

Here *he* is.

This . . . is Bob.

— RJM

PROLOGUE
The Drowning One

I'VE DREAMED OF A new Chronicler.

Some poor sap, broken like me, who might one day take up this cursed quill and let me . . . retire. *Ha.* Dream indeed.

There's a story I've recorded more times than I can count. It begins the same every time: a person in the water, continuously drowning, never dying.

At first, they flail violently, desperately—as if the sea owes them breath. As if the gods might part the waves and grant them reprieve for trying.

But they don't.

There are no gods here. Just salt, silence, and the cruel truth of inevitability.

Sometimes, they sink quickly. Other times, they float—long enough to feel hope, to believe land is near.

Spoiler: it isn't.

And then comes the part I loathe most.

A boat appears—not to rescue, but to watch.

Aboard it: priests, presidents, CEOs. All smiling with teeth like ivory prison bars. They eat. They drink. They sing songs—salvation, patriotism, "working harder." They toss anchors shaped like golden crosses and dollar signs.

They tell the drowning one to hold on.

And they do. Because drowning is terrifying. And maybe—just maybe—they think this is what they deserve.

It isn't. But no one told them that. Not their parents. Not their teachers. Not the ones who lit the fires and taught them to thank them for the warmth as they burned.

I've seen this story scrawled in every tongue—etched into stone, whispered into the void, scratched into skin, sung by blood.

And the ending is always the same: they don't die. They forget what breathing felt like. They become the water.

And me? I keep writing. Because that's what I do, even when I'd rather sleep. Even when the ink is blood, and the truth hurts too much to hold.

They say I chose this. That's true. But not for myself. I chose this—for *him*. Because I know war is coming.

The drowning one will return tomorrow. They always do.

So, too, does history repeat itself.

Maybe . . .

A different face.

But . . .

It's the same story.

The same chains.

And soon—if they agree—*they'll* be the one with the quill.

Ah, that poor fool.

I've watched him for some time now.

Yes, his name is Bob.

I've seen men like him. But he's . . . familiar. Like a mirror I forgot I'd hung on a wall long ago.

The same thoughts, same fears, same silent screams.

I once stood beside him, not physically, but in the places in-between. Interestingly enough, he almost saw me. Almost. He squinted and said something about the sunlight hitting just right.

I see him, and others like him. He fights himself. Every day. He wants to be more. Do more. Yet, the war inside never ceases. I've watched the dam break—its walls crashing down in the flood. I see the layers upon layers of a mask that has been worn thin, but never comes off, and is patched. I've heard the bell toll for him, more than once. He's fragile, almost like a doll that has been continuously reconstructed and deconstructed, weaving a thread that is drawing near its bitter end.

And I—*we*—have a choice.

I could give him purpose—a task, my task. But it would be a heavy sentence—an eternal one. To record the stories no one wants to remember, even as they're lived.

So, I went to Remiel with a proposal.

"He's too broken," Remiel said. "He'll give in and succumb to the darkness. He always does."

I disagreed.

So, we made a wager. If Bob can break his chains and save himself, then I will step aside, and he will take the quill.

And I? I'll help Remiel differently—and in time, who knows what great things will unfold.

Ah, but that's not yet. Remiel smiles—those knowing eyes hiding truths he's not ready to share.

For now, it's the dawn of a brand new day.

And so, we watch. The drowning one returns—different face, same chains.

EPISODE 1: DEATH BECOMES ME

HAVE YOU EVER HAD those moments where you're sitting there (or hell, driving) and just thinking, "Man, I could totally kill myself right now." Or maybe—and work with me here—you're sitting at the dinner table with your family. You know, your spouse, perhaps your parents, kids, siblings, whatever. Then the moment you break bread, you're just like, "Fuck it!" You slam your palms down (or fists, or do a table flip, I don't fucking know), grab that steak knife, and . . . *slit*. You know? Slit your own throat? Literally. Right there. At the dinner table. You got blood spraying, gushing out, dripping down your clothes, all over the furniture, the walls, fine china, the mashed potatoes, on your folks, in your kid's eye. But hey! At least the steak was cooked medium, just how you like it.

Well, if you've ever had moments like these, where you're compelled to do the unthinkable, you're not alone. Hell, I do it all the time. Ladies and gentlemen, allow me to introduce myself. My name is Bob Barnem, and I am a chronic suicidal.

Christ, it sounds like I'm at some AA meeting or in a confessional or something. Yeah, well, I'm not. The truth is, I dunno where I am. I mean, I do; I just don't know where *exactly* I am. I guess I could be dead, dreaming, in a coma. I tried asking others: my wife, my kids, my folks, my friends—hell, even my dog! No one has a goddamn clue what the hell is going on. What I *do* know is this: every time I commit suicide, I'm put right back in bed, safe and cozy.

I suppose I could start by telling you about the first time I had the impulse and why I did what I did.

Now, lemme tell ya, I had no regrets. Not even a letter. I loved my family, an' hell, I still do. It wasn't their fault that I wanted to end it. I was just done—just done with life. I couldn't handle the stress of a transfer out of state, of meeting people who were culturally different, and honestly, of not knowing a single goddamn person. I mean, sure, the pay was good, yeah, but what good is the salary when you bust your balls and ask all the boys at the cooler—"Hey, Pete, Bill, Shaun, guy"—to get a drink after work and don't get a single goddamn word in reply? Instead, they give you this look like, "Who the fuck are you? Oh, it's the new guy!" Bah, fuck 'em. I'll tell you what, those sons of bitches who say that they're there "if you need help," or some "reasonable accommodation," or their "door is always open," they're lying sons of bitches. They don't care about you. They don't care about anyone except their own goddamn selves and their fat fucking wallets.

I do apologize; I seemed to have run off there.

So here's the deal: job transfer out of state. I'm a desk jockey at a firm that deals with the stock market. I have been married for thirteen years, with four kids. I have a lovely house, decent pay, fucked-up neighbors. I got a car, a dog, and some cats. What's there to be wrong? Probably absolutely nothing, and I get that. What happened was pretty simple. I jumped. I jumped right off the roof of the office building and smacked onto the cars and curb below. I say "and curb" because I think—I'm pretty sure, at least—that my feet snapped on it and shattered. I don't know. I can't say I remember anything other than a giant forceful knockout that, well, knocked the shit out of me.

You might be asking, "What were your final thoughts?" Well, for starters: "Oh shit, oh shit, bad idea, bad idea." Followed by, "I'm flying!" Then, "Holy shit, the ground is coming up fast." Next, "Why am I doing this? Who's going to take care of the kids and my wife? What the hell am I doing?" And then, some guilt, anger, sadness, love, happiness. Finally, nothing. *Pow!* Lights out.

Now, hindsight being twenty-twenty, yeah, it was pretty fucking stupid. Do I regret it? Yes and no. Yes, because I was dumb to leave my family alone in this fucked-up world. And no, because, well, I can't die. OK, I can die, but I can't die. I'm like Bill fucking Murray in an extreme, uncensored version of *Groundhog Day*, but it's been going on now for . . . fuck if I know. Either way, nothing is working, and truth be told, I've started to enjoy it. If this is how I get to spend the rest of my days, so be it, I guess. I get to see my wife and kids; that's good enough for me. Still, I can't shake the thought of there being more to this. For now, I'll just get dressed.

By the way, if you haven't figured it out yet—I recently killed myself at the dinner table.

Episode 2: Grand Slam (and My Skull)

Denny's.

Honestly, you can't go wrong with Denny's. On one of my "coming backs," I decided I needed a Grand Slam. Or two, or three—hell, I lost count. Whatever the count was, it was a lot of fucking pancakes, sausage, bacon, eggs. Everything that could give you a heart attack. I think I poured on a good bottle of syrup, too. It's all a bit hazy.

I know, I know, you're probably wondering, "Bob, what the fuck does this have to do with your multiple suicides?" Well, if ya let me finish, I'll be more than glad to tell ya all about it.

So, here I am, sitting at the corner booth in the back. Not a soul around me save for the waitress, who, bless her heart, was so overworked she was probably on the verge of a breakdown. I think her name was Betty. Anyway, I could go on with how she was a young mom, had a cute walk, and all that jazz, but why bother? It wasn't like I'd be seeing her or any of the other sad fucks in there again.

What happened was this: I gave her a hell of an order—one that would make several homeless folks cry with joy. Then I ordered again. And again.

She kept bringing my orders out, and I kept eating. And eating. And eating. Eventually, I ate (and drank) so much that my face smashed right down on the fork, which went into my eye and buried itself deep in my skull. I was diabetic. I guess I still am. I dunno if it was the diabetes—the blood sugar—or maybe my stomach exploded. It wasn't the first time I'd died in this fashion.

Before the darkness descended, I heard her flipping her lid, going on about some hundred-dollar tab going right out the window. Part of me was a bit sad that I'd skipped out on the bill. The other part of me was still just so damn hungry.

In any case, you may be saying, "But Bob, you didn't commit suicide here—you just died." Well, if engorging yourself until you either:

A) Pass out on your fork as a result of all the shit you've eaten on purpose.

B) Fuck you, why do you care?

Honestly, I was just so damn tired of hearing other peoples' problems, which seemed so fucking minuscule in comparison to mine, that I wanted to kill myself again, skip out on the bill, and give everyone a real show.

So, here I am, back in bed. A brand new day is here, ripe for the picking, and, well, I haven't the slightest idea what to do yet. Either way, I'm gonna be around this fucking place for a while.

Jesus Christ, I am so hungry.

Episode 3: Cleanup on Aisle Dead

Part One

So, NOW I BET you're wondering, "Bob, what the hell do you do with all this 'free time' that you have?" Well, a lot of things, really. I mean, I don't always just off myself (or, for you sick fucks out there, get myself off. What the hell's wrong with you?). No, sometimes, I do things to better humanity.

One day, I was on my way to the market. I wanted to take back some beer and soda cans. You know those machines they have that crunch the ever-loving shit out of the cans and bottles? Well, this little shit—must've been around the age of my one boy, Chad—put his favorite stuffed animal in the machine. Everyone's wondering what to do, the kid's screaming his head off, having a meltdown, and the mom's freaking out.

Nobody was doing anything, so I stuck my hand in there and fished around a bit. Apparently, a can was still rolling around in the back. The next thing I knew, I had a hold on the stuffed shit, and then my hand started getting torn to fucking shreds. I had to fight to get my arm back. After I had pulled out (ah-ha, I know), I saw what was left: a stump. I tell ya, there was blood shooting everywhere. I even got some in the kid's eye and all over his mom's chest. There were pieces of the stuffed animal here and there, all good and bloody.

Things went from bad to worse.

Someone nearby just so happened to be trained in the medical field. He took the shirt off his back and started wrapping my "hand," using his belt as a tourniquet. Then I blacked out. I remember being in the back of an ambulance. They were trying to stop the bleeding, but it was no dice. I think we were about two blocks away, and the ambulance got wrecked by a drunk driver who blew through the red light and was speeding.

Thankfully, the guys treating me lived and made it through. Bless 'em for trying. The driver of that old station wagon didn't survive, though, nor did I. But hey, one less drunk on the road, and since I can't die, why not?

I think I had twenty-six bucks in bottles, too. Ah well. Just one of those days, I guess.

Part Two

Another time, I went to the market to get the wife her meds—blood pressure and whatnot. I was in line behind a lot of folks at the counter. Let me paint you a picture: all right, so there's this guy, a big one, huge. He's making a scene and yelling at the clerk about how he can't afford the pills he was prescribed and laying blame on the poor young gal who's just trying to do her job. I'm sure you know the type.

Well, ol' mouth shits here was going off and eventually made her cry. Then the guy started making fun of her. No one did a fucking thing. Now, I'm not one to be chivalrous, but come on! You can't be walking all over someone doing her job, dealing with your raggedy-ass shoving your raging dickheaded nonsense down her throat. No, sir. So, I did what any honest person with balls would do. I found my balls, stepped the fuck up, and told that son of a bitch to calm the fuck down and go take a time out.

Lemme tell ya, telling a grown man to calm the fuck down, let alone a fucking behemoth-sized one, is basically signing your death certificate. But, of course, I couldn't care less. He shifted his anger to me, which was all right. I could take it. Well, I did. Included were a few gallons of water and other fun liquids. So, I took a lot to the face, plus a monitor. That son of a bitch tried to smash my skull in with a fucking monitor! Can you believe that?

Well, dumb ass over here must've never got the memo on what happens when water and electricity mix. Yep, you guessed it. The miserable dumb fuck got his ass shocked to death with me taking the ride. It was pretty fucked up. That's what I got for sticking up for someone. Granted, results may vary, and you might not have a juiced-up, strung-out twat waffle who'll bash your brains in with a fucking monitor, but if the opportunity presents itself, just go for his balls and end it quick.

I've had a lot of bad trips to the supermarket.

Another time, I decided to see what it was like to OD on all the pills. You know, try to live out the high. Man, I gotta tell you, it was some fucking crazy shit. I hallucinated everything imaginable until I blacked out. Have you ever heard of *The Exorcist*? You know, the creepy girl who does the projectile-vomiting shit? Yeah, I was doing that. I would say it was a pretty painful way to go, but honestly, I didn't feel anything coming or going. Choking on my own vomit while I was passed out was a bit lame, but, y'know, these things happen.

Let's see, what else happened? Ah, yeah, I tried to drink the whole liquor aisle. Now, that one took some time. I almost made it, too. Then the cops showed up and arrested me. How did I die? Again, vomit. Fucking vomited in the back seat of the car and croaked. At least I left them assholes a little something special from dear old Bob.

Part Three

Then, I was getting stuff for Memorial Day weekend, which is about as good as Labor Day weekend. The guys would round everyone up, have a bunch of brews, a cookout, the whole shebang. Now, I didn't have anything against it. In fact, I looked forward to it. The last few years before I started killing myself, though, things had been going down the shitter. Fewer folks were coming, and eventually, I had to move away. You know the story—cue the visual montage.

I was gathering stuff up for this weekend's barbecue shitfest at the new place, and, well, I wasn't looking forward to it this time. I was against going to the store with the fam because I had *the* itch. I'd already offed myself in front of them, and I regretted it. Though they'd never remember it, it still struck a nerve with me.

After picking up the charcoal, fluid, and other "fun" items, I wandered around the home goods side. I happened to find those knives for, uh, kitchen use. Well, the itch got to me. I cracked open a package and gave myself a nice new set of lines up and down my forearms and throat. I gotta say, it was a nice contrast—white peppered tile and rich blood. I remember some folks screaming and running, shielding their kids' eyes. That wasn't my fault. They dragged their kids along to fucking gawk at me, twitching and dying. Who the fuck does that?

Before I blacked out, I saw a guy put down a Floor Slippery When Wet cone. I'm unsure if that final laugh escaped, but thanks, kid. You made a dead guy laugh.

I guess I could have gone to sporting goods, gotten a rifle or a handgun, maybe even a hunting knife. But that would have been a little more complicated, and someone probably would have thwarted my attempt.

Another trip in, since it was a "soft reset," I got all the shit I needed, avoided the knives, and made my way over to the deli to get some fried chicken for lunch. I still had that itch, though. It was gonna be a long fucking day.

I got over there and looked at all the great food. Usually, my mouth would be so wet it'd make my throat orgasm. It wasn't this time, maybe because of the itch. Don't know, don't care. At any rate, I went into autopilot mode, and that was that. I went over to a deep fryer, shoved a few people out of the way, and just slammed my face nice and deep in that vat of hot oil—for a good twenty or so seconds. Eventually, I just kind of slid in a little bit and died. I might add that my head was good and fried to a golden brown. Yeah, this one hurt like a motherfucker.

Reset.

We're back at the store. Well, this time around, I got the hunger itch. So, I got to thinking about all that cereal and all that candy in one giant fucking aisle. It's a wet dream come true. So, this one's for you diabetics, kids, and curious folk everywhere. I grabbed a few gallons of milk, grabbed the candy, grabbed the cereal, and just ate and ate and fucking ate that shit up like succotash. It was an enlightening experience. Until I got all jittery and started throwing up. Milk, cereal, vomit, and candy do not taste good together, lemme tell ya.

Well, because of my diabetes and whatnot, I ended up passing the fuck out, choking on my fucking vomit again, and dying in awe-inspiring decoupage of gluttony.

Another reset, but that part's boring. It was an alright weekend, but I think I could have had more fun at the market. Those damn morals get in the way of really having fun. I'm just not that psychotic.

EPISODE 3.5: STARS, STRIPES, AND SUICIDE ATTEMPTS

"HAPPY INDEPENDENCE DAY, FOLKS." Or, as it really is, 'Wear-Your-USA-Flag-Bikini Day and Shoot Shit Off All Fucking Day.' Yay!

Heaven forbid you try to get to sleep early because you've got a job—one that demands you're up before the damn rooster starts his screeching solo. Or maybe you're not wearing your Old Navy flag shirt. Perhaps you're not into your house shaking like it's under siege at one in the goddamn morning while your dog has a meltdown and your pops starts prepping for Vietnam: Round Two.

But yeah, somehow, *you're* the inconsiderate, un-American one.

Hardly anyone remembers what the Fourth of July is supposed to be about anymore. These days? It's PTO, patriot cosplay, and pyrotechnic pissing contests. Crack a Bud Light, light a Roman candle, and scream "MURICA!" like you discovered freedom in the clearance bin at Walmart.

This year's goal? Be the absolute asshole neighbor. I planned to shoot off everything I could get my hands on until the cops showed up or the timeline reset—whichever came first. Let's call it pulling an Uno reverse card on my usual brand of depression.

The boss wanted a get-together at my place, so we had people over—neighbors, friends, coworkers I barely tolerated, and random folks drawn by the smell of overcooked burgers, hot dogs, and beer. I wanted solitude and time with my family, not a party, but I slapped on a "God Bless America" smile and played host.

The day started off fine: no death itch, just enough anxiety to float a parade float—classic American barbecue vibes. People lined up to see who had the biggest firework and the smallest sense of mortality. That's when it hit me: *I hate the Fourth of July.*

So, we gathered for a fireworks showdown. After enduring the "who has the bigger boom" contest, I decided it was my turn. Save the best for last, right?

I stood up, strolled to the launcher, and prepped the payload. I figured it was time to give 'em a show they would remember. Everyone was watching—every eye on dear old Bob. Well, except for the kids, who were inside, hypnotized by video games—can't blame 'em.

Then, right on cue, the neighbors on the other street kicked off *their* pyro-palooza. It felt like I was now trapped in a goddamn Creedence Clearwater Revival tribute reel ripped straight from social media—nothing like having your thunder stolen and your cereal pissed in.

The dogs were barking more, and the babies were screaming even louder. People were laughing like they'd never known pain. Hell, I had some jackass put his arm around me, spill beer on my foot, and call it "patriotic."

I decided to contribute to the mayhem. My way, naturally. I figured let's make this go 0-100 even faster than the guy in the corner that shotgunned one way too beers.

I rigged together a bouquet of M-80s with enough electrical tape to qualify as an OSHA violation, dropped it into Ted's DIY mortar launcher, and lit the fuse like I was christening the U.S.S. Trauma.

Have you ever seen *Mission Impossible*, where the fuse sizzles and maybe your sphincter clenches? Perhaps that's just me. Anyway, yeah, it's like that. Except I shortened the fuse because I knew someone would try to be a hero. Lo and behold, someone did, but they were too slow.

The boom came, and I opened my mouth. What a load, I tell ya. Caught the fireworks straight to the face—a screaming, red-white-and-blue finale. POP goes Bob.

When the day reset—yep, still can't die—I figured, why not keep the party going?

First, a fistful of M-80s—plenty painful. Messy. Effective. At least no one tried to be a hero. Next, a bunch of firecrackers—swallowed them whole. Hoo, what a spicy meatball, I tell you.

You're thinking, "Bob, that's impossible." It's not. I don't recommend it. Lost a hand and got my insides torn up more than some hentai fetish fuckwits debating on "rearranging some waifu's guts." You can't see it, but I'm shaking my head. Fuck, the internet has gotten weird.

Anyway, those were the fun ones. Then, there were some resets where there was some grilling.

In one, the family and I decided on a cookout. I thought, "Why not?" Then, everyone started launching fireworks all at once. The dogs were barking, the cats were losing it, and the kids were screaming—a full-on clusterfuck.

I'd had enough. Sure, *everyone else* was having a blast, but old Bob? Nah. I was done. I'd just put the burgers on the grill when it happened. It was automatic, I'd say. Then again, it wasn't the first time I went "fuck it" and did what I wanted. So, Bob's burgers are sizzling; I wandered over to the garage, grabbed the gas can, walked to the street, doused myself, then flicked my lighter and toasted myself to a Happy 4th.

People just stood there, stunned. Their quiet neighbor turned into a Roman candle. I'd stuffed firecrackers in my pockets for added pizzazz and glamor. I would say I was beautiful. Self-barbecue? It's not what it's cracked up to be. Hurts like hell. I don't recommend it. Eventually, your brain flips the off-switch, and your body hits well done. Me? I was more medium. Maybe . . . medium-well.

But that was just one take.

I was somewhere else each time, with a different way to check out. Onetime, I took special care to rig an M-80 into a car's gas tank and drive it straight into a creek, blasting Foghat's *Slow Ride* on the stereo.

The other was at Sid's, where I made an M-80 vest. Ha, I walked into the yard like Uncle Sam's suicidal sidekick. Boom. I lit up like the goddamn Macy's finale.

At Jerry's, I crafted some makeshift cherry bombs and hid them in the beer as I sipped it. Boom—face and hand gone.

Then there was Terry's. We went into the woods. I told the guys I had as how for them, something real magical. They laughed it off.

"Alright, Bob. Can't wait," they said.

I'd strapped fireworks to *everything*. My arms. My legs. My ass. Lit the fuse and gave them a send-off they'll probably never forget. Well, I won't, at least. Some of them screamed. A few of them laughed. Most just stared in stunned silence. You come to know who your real friends are. *Hint: It was the ones that laughed.*

In the end, though, something strange happened. The last time was when I wasn't itching to off myself, I decided to spend the time with my family and enjoy it. Crazy, I know.

That night, my wife and I got into a coupling session, you know, that good old post-hot-dog coitus. In the end, it was a good day—hardly anyone shot their shit off. Well, except for me. Still, that's pretty sweet, right? But later, as the night rolled into the 5th, I ended up dying in my sleep.

Before I died, I had a dream. It felt like a rerun, but I wasn't just watching—I was in it. There was a girl, maybe in high school, and I think I was mugging her. I don't know why, so don't ask. She didn't panic. She knew how it'd play out. She pulled out a deck of cards and shuffled like the devil's own magician.

What was it she said? Something like, "All life is a gamble."

Then she dealt me my hand in that grimy alleyway: an ace of clubs and spades, an eight of clubs and spades, and a ten of spades. A Dead Man's Hand. Real fucking cute. Before I could react, the hand holding the gun exploded, and my face damn near dissolved. It wasn't glamorous, to say. Then she gathered her cards, gave a creepy smile, and vanished into the night. Then I woke up to wherever and whenever I am now.

Weird shit, I tell ya.

Yeah, yeah, you're thinking, "Wow, Bob, you didn't kill yourself?" I was amazed, too. It was the only Fourth where I didn't kill myself. At least, not on purpose.

Still, at least I shot my rocket off, and it ended up being a happy ending. That counts, right?

So, happy Independence Day, folks. Don't blow your face off—unless you're into that sort of thing.

Me? I blew mine off six times before dessert.

I think the universe is trying to tell me something. I just hope it speaks my language.

Bob's Fireworks Safety Tip #1: Don't Do This.

Just . . . don't. Unless you've got a death loop clause and no shame, in that case, carry on, patriot.

Episode 4: The Road to Nowhere (and Back Again)

Part One

Hidy ho, folks. I'm back and here to spread the good word. What word, you ask? Well, death, of course. More specifically, suicide: hanging, slit wrists, gunshot wounds (head to toe), trains, planes, and, of course, automobiles!

So, there I was driving down US-127, and a thought came to my mind: I wonder what it's like to hit that median going full out? And then, I wonder what it's like to hit a utility pole, a tree, that huge-ass puddle of standing water full-speed-ahead, Captain? The one that kept creeping on me, though, was, I wonder what it's like to get hit by a Mack Truck.

I mean, sure, the Internet has loads of clips and lovely photos for your scrapbook. But you don't know how it feels. That was the ticket for me. There was no one in the car with me. I mean, I am an asshole, but not the kind of twat who would kill himself and then leave his wife and kids to scream (and probably die) while he enjoyed his demise again. So, you sick fucks get that thought out of your minds.

What happened was I pulled over to the side of the road. I even did that whole courtesy thing, putting on the hazard lights and stuff. Then I got out and made it seem like I was getting ready to change my tire or pop the hood. Unfortunately, some guy stopped to help me out. I told the guy no thanks and that I was okay. Well, I guess he was a do-gooder or something because he was pretty damn adamant about helping out dear old Bob.

Honestly, it made me want to die a lot quicker. So, I took note of the semi coming up real fast. I had to time it right, though, ya see, because I didn't want to give the guy much time to stop, let alone alert other drivers that I had a death wish.

'Big Bertha' and I got acquainted real quick. Pow! Right in the kisser, the jewels, everything. I kissed that grill pretty well and gave that old girl a new paint job.

I felt sorry for the guy who tried to help, bless his goody-two-shoes heart. He attempted to stop me. And his kids saw a random guy go splat all over the interstate. The bottom line is to be careful who you try to help out. If someone wants to die, they're going to find a way.

By the way, if you're wondering what I felt when I got smashed to mush, the answer is nothing much—just a whole lot of force, a brief sensation of pain, and then lights out.

Part Two

"Bob, why are you so selfish? Doing all these heinous acts and subjecting people to this kind of nonsense?" I know this is what you're thinking.

Well, guess what? It ain't your life or your story to tell, bub. That's what. Besides, I already said that I regret that my kids, my wife, my parents, and so on and on and fucking on watched me die—the people who mattered and the innocents I kind of ruined. But hey, if they don't see it now, they'll do it themselves one day, or they'll find one of their friends hanging from a beam in the middle of a room or with his throat slit, gunshot to his head out in a field, dead in a bathtub with a toaster. Face it, folks: it's the real world. These things can and do happen.

Now, I wouldn't say that this is an educational story or whatever. Well, maybe it is. But let me get back on track.

As I said before, I get these itches, and I had one while driving down Main Street. This time, the thought was, I *wonder what it's like to hit a tree? Just full out.* Trees are pretty tough old broads. They've been around for a while, right? I drove down the street and found one that I liked on the edge of town. Hell, I even got out and looked 'er over. Located a few couples' names carved into the bark. Ha!

I got back in the car, drove back into town, and waited until the night had settled in good and well. I started going in fast and caught the attention of a local cop. Props, indeed. The guy was doing his job. Tax dollars at work—I was glad to see it in action. I flew around that bend and found that tree. I met that sappy bastard right quick.

For added effect, I hadn't done up my seat belt. And, well, in short, that sucked. A lot. The force of hitting the tree wasn't what did me in. It was going over the steering wheel, getting caught on it, smashing through the windshield, smacking the hood of the car and the tree, and then breaking an arm between the tree and the vehicle. Yeah. That was a lot of fucking fun. Five out of five would never do that again.

Honestly, it was more painful than when I did the same thing except with my seat belt on. And this time, it was a telephone pole, not a tree. The same cop, though. Nice guy. He was there until the end. I oughta write his precinct and say he deserves a commendation. Anyway, the results of the three telephone pole incidents are as follows:

Outcome one (and two): My insides became a stew—broken ribs and sternum, snapped neck, bleeding on the brain, and Jell-O for brains. ~~Bill Cosby would approve~~[1]. That was all before the electric line came down and started a fire. The first time, I was trapped and burned to a crisp. The second time, I was pulled out and pronounced dead on the spot due to all the internal bleeding and shit.

Outcome three: No seat belt, so see results of tree-hugging above, except that more limbs got bent, and I took out a few blocks of power.

I know these aren't as exciting as kissing a Mack Truck. And I got some more bad news for ya, folks: ramming a brick wall ain't that impressive either.

So, there's an abandoned factory in town, right? It was just sitting there doing nothing. I couldn't go balls out, flooring it through town to get to it, though, so I improvised. I led the cops on a little chase around the block. You know the kind—Joker style, the Heath Ledger one, with that one scene. Anyway, once I had their attention and knew no one was going to be following (mostly), I drove straight to the factory. I made my sprint across the parking lot, hit that wall, and down it all came.

---

1. Bob doesn't condone rape or drugging other people to rape them. Bob thinks that's fucked up. Bob is also referring to the old Jell-O commercial. Please, don't blame Bob.

That's right. I came for a brick wall, and I got the whole shebang. A good portion of that factory landed on me, but it was all right. My trial concluded. I reached a verdict: never again would I ram a brick wall or any building. It turns out suffocating is one of my least favorite ways to go. But hey, it's all part of the learning experience.

Part Three

So, I've hugged a few trees, kissed a few telephone poles, and rammed a brick wall. I bet you're wondering, "Bob, what the hell is wrong with you? Why all the self-hate and being a menace to society?" Well, Jack—if one of you's name is Jack (and it probably is)—if I wanted to sound like a fucking broken record, I'd record all this and leave it playing on a loop for eternity. It'd make those ten or hundred hours of Epic Sax Guy look like nothing. Not that I have anything against Epic Sax Guy. It's just you can only take so much until your head pops. As for being a menace to society, just look at your election and what the news outlets want to keep you distracted from. There's a whole lot more menacing out there than your dear old Bob.

On my many adventures in finding out the best way to die via motor vehicle, I learned that driving off a cliff is an exotic way to go. Great stuff. Ten out of ten. I would do it again. In fact, I did it a few times. It's like a rollercoaster and that gut-in-your-mouth feeling. You expect that sudden jerking motion to pull you back up, but it never does. Instead, you plummet X number of feet to your death. You get tossed around like a dummy (pun intended) that missed the fucking crash wall and is just flailing his arms like some crazed lunatic.

Meanwhile, while you're flailing around like said lunatic, your insides are getting crushed by the sheer force, and no matter how fucking soft you think your seats are, your ass is broken. Your Jell-O brain is soup—a bloody soup at that—while your insides are a hearty stew that's literally stewing. You're an oversized Ziploc container of man stew.

Now, you'd be lucky if one of those forceful jerks along the way down knocked you out (no slow dying). That's a luxury, though. It's all about chance, really. With each thud you're making in the car, you're pulling off the top of the deck, hoping by that time, you'll have passed the fuck out. Never mind that you could potentially burst into flames, get barbequed, and/or start a fire that burns a bit of the forest. Ah, the shit that happens.

Another idea occurred to me during one of my many plummets down the side of . . . whatever mountain it was: I always wanted to fly like Superman. Take to the skies, be a hero. It reminds me of a dream I had of flying. I even met another flying guy, and we both did a double-take. Anyway, I went driving off a cliff without a seatbelt on. Hell, you can even plant a heavy-ass rock, cinder block, whatever, on the accelerator, cling to the roof, let go—and just fly.

Now, you're in for a real treat here, folks. Because you're not gonna get tossed about inside a metal can anymore. Oh no, you're gonna be kissing a lot of things with your mouth. And your ass. And while you're kissing every boulder, rock, shrub, tree, and God knows what else on your trip down the mountain, you're gonna be wishing that you stayed in that car. Granted, some trees won't give, and you'll just splatter against them. The problem is that you might still be alive when you finally land. Then, a hungry wild animal that loves some fresh meat comes wandering by. Circle of life, I suppose.

So, there you have it. Driving off cliffs by dear old Bob.

I guess I'll throw in the honorable mention. One time, when I was going to drive off a cliff, I had a change of heart—it was weird, really. I bailed and skidded on the pavement for a reasonable distance since, you know, I wanted to "go the distance" when I went off the side of the cliff. Well, I got acquainted with the pavement, and she ground me down to bits and pieces, to chunks and a long-ass red streak on the highway. I wouldn't recommend kissing the curb either, folks.

Episode 5: Snap, Crackle, Pop—My Neck

Part One

YOU KNOW THAT CEREAL made by Kellogg's? Ah, what was it called? No, not the anti-masturbation one. Well, I suppose most were. Oh yeah, Rice Krispies. Yeah, that's it. It had those three characters: Snap, Crackle, and Pop. Well, I have a funny story for ya.

So, you know how I get these itches, right? Well, this time, I wanted to know what it'd be like to hang myself. Simple enough, really, right? I thought so. But maybe I was just doing it all wrong.

The idea is that you make the noose, put your noggin through it, and kick out the chair or whatever you used to stand on. Let me paint you the picture. The kids and wife are gone away, and I'm home alone. I know, I know—now you think that they all came back and found "dear old dad" swinging in the archway.

Uh, no. Because I thought I'd also try out one of those suicide helplines. Don't get me wrong—they worked pretty hard to talk me down. But then I informed them that it didn't matter and that I was going to die. Oh, and also that it wasn't their damn decision if I wanted to take my life or not. Picture me swinging, giving you a "double fuck you" as hard as I can before the lights go out.

Anyway, I was stringing myself up in the archway. I told the helpline to call the cops so that they could cut me down before the wife and kids got home. Well, the first time, it didn't go exactly as planned. My neighbor, bless 'em, saw me hooking up with the rope and decided to be a hero.

Now, don't get me wrong, I like it when folks go all good an' stuff, but I don't need Nickelback coming to rescue my ass if I want to get myself off. Speaking of which . . . I need to add that to my to-do list.

Anyway, so the guy comes in and gets me down. While I'm flailing about, just trying to die in peace, I end up falling and breaking my arms. Two loud *pops*, a few *crackles*, and some *snaps*. Yeah, that felt wonderful. If I weren't already dead so many times over, and if I gave a damn, I'd have sued that guy. But ya move on and just try it at different places.

I figured that maybe I could go out to the woods not too far from the house. It has a creek, which led me to think that the sound of running water could mask the sound of someone gasping for air. I found a big ol' oak tree and set myself up. The first time, the branch wasn't thick enough to support my ass. The next limb did just swell. I tried this a few times, moving on to more dramatic "jump n' hang" sessions.

Swaying there as life leaves you, you get a few good moments of realizing that this isn't a great way of going out. There's plenty of time to realize that you fucked up. And remember where you placed the remote. Then poof. Darkness. It's a slow way to go—like a snail's pace.

The jumping made it a bit interesting. I climbed up above the branch and just leaped. I tell ya, my neck snapped like a Slim Jim. It hurt for a moment, but that moment was so quick I woke up back in my bed, ready for round two. The other time, though, my neck didn't snap cleanly, and I was left dangling there like a testicle that had popped out of someone's briefs, swaying in the breeze. After that, I decided it was time to try appeasing the itch another way.

Part Two

Have you ever wondered what it'd be like to fall down the stairs and snap your neck? Maybe you did it as a kid—the falling down the stairs bit. Perhaps it was a marvel that you didn't kill yourself if you were born in the nineties or earlier. I ain't gonna sugarcoat it: I feel that kids today are so damn spoiled. They've lost the thrill of going outside and getting dirty. It just bothers me.

Anyway, I always liked doing somersaults down the stairs. Y'know, being a fucking tumbleweed. Later in life, though, I started thinking of making it seem like those damn stairs just had it out for me. You know that line in cartoons or classic movies: "Watch out, that last step is a doozy?" You get the picture.

Alright, so, I took a few spills in the home—on a long set of stairs. The short ones do minimal damage. At the time, life was rough. I was in a bad spot and thought it'd probably be better if I were out of the picture. The wife and I were at each other's throats. The medication the docs had prescribed wasn't doing much for me, and, well, I'd had about enough of it. So, I made sure my insurance policy was still up to date and checked the amount: $500,000. Not bad. I mean, then, at least she'd have a lovely house. She'd be better off without me. I mean, yeah, I'd miss her and our child (we just had one at the time), but eh, I wasn't myself.

I had to make sure it looked like an accident—faulty stairs or handrail, lousy step, or just an "oops" moment. Three out of four attempts on those stairways to Heaven, if you will, were successful. I also tried adding some flair—jazz hands, mimicking the Wilhelm scream (even playing it), and a few other things.

The critical thing to remember is that you'll live through most, if not all, of the tumble. It's not an easy task, nor is it fun. It hurts. A lot. So, with each spill, I'm breaking my wrist, leg(s), ankle(s), arm(s), and maybe, just maybe, my neck. Lying there at the foot of the stairs with bones popping out of my ankle, wrist, arm—not too fucking pleasant, I'll tell ya what. I became a giant wad of paper. An oversized wad of bloody meat paper.

However, if your loved ones are left behind less financially burdened, well, it's an excellent choice. Most companies void the insurance policy in the case of suicide, y'know.

Episode 6: Cutting Out the Middleman

Part One

ANOTHER DAY, ANOTHER DOLLAR. I hate what corporate America has become. Of course, I used to hate it so much that I eventually took my life as a result. The American Dream isn't what it used to be. It's gone astray, warped, a disease that infects us from deep within and causes us to roam and live paycheck to paycheck. Fuck you cunts at the top and your bullshit golden shower trickle-down economics. Also, fuck you to the people who bought into that.

I used to get so worked up about it that I cut myself. But I had to make sure I kept it hidden. I couldn't afford to be tossed into the loony bin. I couldn't deal with the idea of my wife leaving me and taking my kids away. Or having folks come in and say that I was unfit to be a father and that they were gonna place my kids in a foster home or some shit.

So, I'd cut myself on my thighs, my armpits, between my toes, below the waistline, and a few other places. Eventually, as times got harder to cope with and I was making preparations for my demise, I stopped caring about where I cut myself. So, I started cutting my forearms in elaborate designs. I figured, hell, why not?

After killing myself the first time, I came to cutting once again. But a lot of the scars wouldn't heal. A reminder or a joke? Either way, I wasn't gonna let it stop me from doing what I was doing best here.

One day, I needed something to fix the sink, so I went to the old hardware store in town—you know, the mom-and-pop kind of deal. Well, I walked in and saw a pretty little thing, thought some bad thoughts, cracked a grin to myself, and wandered on. I got some guy to help me select something I could use to either fix the situation permanently or temporarily. I chose the short route—I ain't no handyman. I hate the idea of getting all dirty trying to fix something and then fucking it up further.

I was looking at all the shiny merchandise and happened to find the hammers, saws, etc. Well, I ended up getting an itch. So, there I was down aisle five, taking a hammer to my fingers. The thuds were loud. The blood poured all over me. And on the floor. A guy tried to stop me. Hell, even that pretty little thing cried out, too. I decided to go the maniacal route and "attack" them, only to further injure myself. Eventually, they tried to overpower me, and I figured, "If the hammer's gonna fall, it's gonna be by my hand." So, I brought the claw down on my skull a few times—the human will! With a grin, I dropped to the ground and watched the lights slowly dim.

I couldn't help but think of that teapot song: "Here is my hammer, and here is my skull. When I bring it down and smash about, watch all my blood and brains spill out."

Part Two

Whenever I'd get to cutting, I'd sometimes notice another feeling lingering deep within. I couldn't ever quite put my finger on it. It seemed like an impulse—another kind of urge. Some thirst I couldn't quite sate. Times were getting pretty bad for dear old Bob.

He reached for a jagged piece of glass and proceeded to make slits in his face. Blood poured through the precise cuts and dripped onto the concrete. People stared on, bewildered, shocked—in awe of the man who had put his fist and head through the shop window moments ago.

The man known as Bob looked around, wildly grinning, his blood-soaked gaze taking in the busy street that had come to a standstill. He hadn't quite had a feeling like this before. It gave him a rush. There was something else, though. Something deep within told him to turn that glass shard on the people. He had always been at war with himself, but this time—this time, it was worse than anything he could remember.

A dark blue-uniformed police officer ran up to the crowd, his weapon drawn. "Sir, I need you to put down the weapon!"

Bob laughed hysterically. He then proceeded to cut off the rest of his face and hold it up before the crowd. The officer advanced, as did others, hoping to be heroes in another's eyes. Hastily, Bob slit his wrists and his throat before attempting to chew and swallow the broken shards of glass.

Then he lay on the sidewalk, decrepit, bloody, and broken. The urge to kill others had passed. He was sated only by taking his own life.

After that, I woke up in my bed. The scars were still visible—to me, anyway. Yes, it is hard to slit both your wrists. Impossible? No. I call it dedication. This time, though, I was worried.

EPISODE 7: A CUT ABOVE THE REST

Part One

AFTER THAT LAST INCIDENT, I got to wondering. What was happening to me? What was I becoming? Was whatever that was going on here, with me, my deaths—was it all starting to spiral out of control? Was I losing what was left of my humanity? Of my sanity? The feelings I'd had when surrounded by all those people: They were unhealthy. They weren't me. I knew it. But I so badly wanted to act on them. Kill.

I couldn't forget that feeling. I couldn't shake it off. It was haunting me, and I knew . . . I knew something was going on. But I just didn't know what.

I got out of bed and wandered around the house. The wife and kids weren't anywhere to be found, just a note. They'd gone to the store. I figured I'd go for a drive somewhere. Maybe go into town and take a walk down by the pond. I used to go there when I'd get batshit crazy. I figured it'd do me some good.

Well, it didn't quite go as planned.

Bob wandered around the pond. He'd change benches here and there every so often. He couldn't find that "right spot" to chill out and calm his troubled mind.

A glimmer in the grass caught his eye as he walked along the sidewalk. He walked over and inspected the knife. It was a basic hunting knife. No different from those he saw at the stores he frequented. This one, however, was so alluring. Warm. Inviting. A tool for hunting. Cooking. And murder.

Memories of the prior event came back, full-on surging, flowing throughout his entire being. He needed to quench his bloodthirst. Somehow, someway. *Maybe, just maybe, if I can't die, there are no repercussions for me?* Bob thought about this for a moment. He looked at the knife, wielding it as if he were about to drive it deep into someone's neck, with the intent to take a life. He could see his reflection in it. A slight grin turned into a sadistic, gleeful smile.

He acted fast. Plunged the blade deep into the side of his neck. Blood spurted across the sidewalk and onto the grass. People screamed and fled while others rushed to save the hapless bastard. Bob lay there dying, frightened. Frightened for the first time in a long, long time. Slowly, the day's warm orange glow faded to black. Sounds of car engines roaring and feet stamping on concrete faded to nothing.

He went back to what he knew best. Nothing.

Bob woke on a bench in the park. A scar on his neck told the story of what had just transpired. No one noticed him, at first, anyway, until he sat up and stared down at his hands. The knife had remained.

"What the hell is going on?"

Part Two

As Bob sat holding the knife, he felt the itch return again. It gnawed at him. First, at his mind. Then his arm. And then his hand. It felt like he was being piloted and driven by someone else.

Then he was in town. He was walking with an energy, a dark kind, fueled by some unknown source, where he was lured to an alleyway. He heard gasps and muffled screams. A struggle! He didn't bother to creep down the alley. He knew what he had to do.

He came around the corner and saw a man holding down a woman at knifepoint, trying to take her pants off. Some passersby ignored the spectacle, some hurried past, others lazily watched.

Bob was disgusted and enraged. He came up behind the man and picked him up. "You think it's OK to rape, you sick fuck?"

"Woah, woah, what's your deal, man," asked the rapist.

"You make me sick." He spat the words out. "You all make me fucking sick. Especially those of you who're getting your rocks off. The fuck is the matter with you!"

The others scurried out of the alleyway. Sirens were approaching fast.

"Listen, pal—"

Bob drove his knife into the man's gut.

"I ain't your pal, guy." Bob stared deep into the eyes of the filth.

The woman scrambled to her feet and ran. By the time she reached the alleyway entrance, the cops had arrived.

"You know, this isn't so bad. I kind of like it," said Bob, a big grin on his face.

"The fuck is wrong with you, man?" said the rapist, clutching his gut.

"You—all of you sick fucks. Taking advantage of the system of people, preying on the weak and innocent. Ya know what? Prey on my knife." Bob snarled, almost demonic-like, and began to plunge the knife repeatedly into the man's gut, dragging it in all sorts of directions.

The man collapsed, his blood and insides covering the concrete of the alleyway.

"Put your hands up where we can see them!" an officer shouted.

Bob ignored the command and stood over the fast-dying man. "I bet you'd have shot me already if I was black!" Bob quipped.

"Put. The. Knife. DOWN!"

"Fuck you!"

"Sir, put the weapon down and get on the ground!"

"You can try, but you won't take me alive, copper," said Bob to himself.

"Put the knife down!"

"Never."

"Put it down!"

"Never."

"Put the fucking knife down—now dammit!"

"I said, never!" And then Bob charged at an officer.

The cops unloaded their guns on the poor sap known as Bob. He smiled and laughed as he stared up at them from the ground, feeling the familiar sensation leave him—only to return a few moments later.

It was something new, let me tell ya. That fucker had it coming, though. I can't say I'm exactly proud to have killed someone, but no one else would've done anything to help that gal. Hell, I probably could have gotten the two guys who were watching and wanking to it as well. To Hell with 'em all.

I am hoping that this itch goes away, though. I mean, something's got to give. Right?

Part Three

So, I've had this knife for a little while now. I dunno what its deal is, but it seems to be constantly calling out to me. Whenever I'm near it, I get the itch to take a life—and my own isn't satisfying its thirst. I thought I could be a decent kind of a guy, ya know? But I don't know how long I can hold out if I'm doomed.

I can't get rid of it. It keeps appearing in my hands or pockets. It's just there. Maybe it's an extension of me? The darkness and hunger that has always been there? Something. What I do know is that this is my burden, and I have to carry it forever.

Another thing I have to deal with is the scars. People can see me clear as day, and they see a fuck-ugly guy with scars on his face, neck, hands, and arms—it's so disgusting even I can't stomach it. So, I'm gonna go on over to the museum. I mean, if there's something there that could give me an idea about what this knife may be, shoot, I'm all for it.

Bob made his way down the busy city streets to the museum downtown. He figured he'd probably get questions about the knife when he went through the metal detector, but it never showed up or wasn't noticeable to the guards. Perhaps it was chance—maybe this was the path he would take to find the truth he sought.

He approached a woman at a counter under a prominent sign that read "Information." She was young, attractive, and had a voice that helped put him at ease.

"How may I help you," she asked.

Bob adjusted, took a breath, and released his strange query. "Well, ya see, I have an artifact that I'd like to have looked at. I was wondering if you could point me in the direction of having someone look at it, by chance?"

Her eye held a peculiar look. Something supernatural was at work, but he couldn't make it out. It was a look he was starting to see in some people. Folks who had a dark secret or had made a bargain with . . . something.

"Ah, why yes. I can page the curator, and he'll have someone meet with you in the backroom, down the hall on the left." The woman was calm. Ridiculously calm.

Bob smiled and gave a slight nod. He had turned his back and started the other way when he heard her say, "Have a nice day . . . Bob." He turned around. The woman was gone. His heart sank. Was this some kind of game? Someone's twisted manipulation of reality? Was he going to wake up being jacked into a machine? Was he dead and just in some kind of Hell? Questions flooded the poor sap's head, and he had no one to give him any answers—except possibly someone at the end of the hall on the left, in the back room.

The curator was terribly old, with almost as many wrinkles as Father Time. Bob nearly mistook him for Death. Dressed all in black, he had a broad chin and a bushy white beard that had grown to mid-chest. Short white hair hid under his black professor hat. Behind his tiny spectacles, his eyes were bright with the blue of an ever-clear sky.

The man spoke with a soothing voice. It possessed something that Bob hadn't felt in a long-time—comfort. "Ah, good day, sir." Though he appeared frail, he stepped lightly and with assurance and had a hell of a handshake. "I trust you are here to discuss this relic you possess."

"Yeah, I have this knife . . ." Bob retrieved the ordinary-looking blade from his pocket. "I can't quite say how I came into its possession. It . . . I . . . we kinda found each other."

The curator took the blade and examined it. "Ah, interesting." He looked up at Bob and then back at the knife. "Well, I am not often gifted with such a find."

"What do you mean?" Bob asked, his interest piqued. "What is it?"

"This is the Kris of Judas. Also known as the Knife of the Betrayer. Contrary to its name, it actually has no affiliation with Judas or the betrayal of Christ. The scholars who first discovered it dubbed it so. In a sense, it has existed for countless lifetimes; its appearance constantly changes."

Bob rubbed his brow in confusion.

The curator nodded. "It's quite puzzling, isn't it? That's what makes it so fascinating, though!"

Bob stared at the knife and then at the curator. "Well, I just want to get rid of it. If you want it for your museum, you can have it."

"You're too kind, sir. However, that would be against the rules. You see, this is not my burden to bear. It is yours." The curator returned the knife to Bob and cleaned his tiny spectacles with a white cloth.

"What? What are you talking about? What do you mean, rules and burden?" Bob grew hysterical. "I just wanna go back—I wanna go back and live my life. Be free."

"Ah, you thought this was all a charade, right? Perhaps a dream within a dream—some intricately planned inception?" The man's voice hinted at something darker. "You're new here. I can understand your lack of comprehension. Though, I suppose, it has been quite a long, long time since I've been here. Alas, as you can see, I've adapted and become an instrument in . . . educating and calculating events. A sort of chronicler, if you will."

Bob stared at the man, dumbfounded. "Who . . . what are you? Wh—Where am I?"

The old man smiled. "You exist in reality. And you keep jumping to different universes in which you exist. Your mind, the present you, keeps integrating itself into your parallel bodies. And since you believe you are in limbo, well, you can see . . ."

Bob's gaze dropped to the ground, following his heart. "So, I really am dead?

"Where you initially existed?" The curator was seemingly holding back a grin and paused for a moment. "Yes, you are. But here, you are alive."

Bob needed more answers. "What about the 'itches' I get? What about the sudden impulses to kill people?"

"Those are hardwired impulses. We're all capable of things, Bob. Sometimes we can ignore them, the urges, or as you call them, 'itches.' Other times, well, that's how we get murderers, rapists, criminals, etc. Now, I'm not saying it's hard-coded in your DNA—it's just that you are animals. You are beasts, cursed flesh beings with needs and wants. You lust after looks and salivate over the temptation of what could be instead of cherishing what you have now, whether bad or good. You claim selflessness when, in fact, your kind is so selfish that it can laugh at a dying person and mock him as he takes his final breath. Your religious zealotry is quite astounding as well."

The old man laughed. "Ah, I could ramble on and on about what I see wrong with your race, Bob. I suppose I could say that it's not entirely your fault—humanity's really—but in some aspects, it is. Every choice and every action has a consequence. This, what you are experiencing, is your consequence."

Bob stood in awe and felt sick at the same time.

"How does it feel to be a remnant of a memory? Of a life, someone else lived?"

"I . . . I don't know what to think," replied Bob.

"Give it time. You seem to be on the right path, minus having killed yourself in countless universes so far. You keep that up, and you won't wake up one day."

"What happens then?" asked Bob.

The old man made elaborate, open-armed gestures. "Welcome to the void!" He laughed. "Now, I suggest you take your relic and keep searching—not for answers, but for yourself."

"What do you mean keep searching for myself?"

"You've answered enough questions, Chronicler," said a deep voice from within the room. "Your task is done. Thank you for your service."

Bob then found the knife buried deep in the old man's chest.

"What! What the hell!" Bob cried, panic rising as he looked over the old man who was now dead—by his knife.

"We will get you, Bob," repeated the voice. "You will not escape us. Not for long."

The voice shook Bob to his core. He had never felt so much fear and dread in his life. Not ever. He dislodged the knife and ran from the room.

Wraiths impeded his progress down each corridor: mist-like dark figures with fiery red eyes fixated on him. All misshapen, disfigured, familiar scars and wounds, like they'd died thousands of deaths.

The people in the museum were oblivious to them and Bob.

"There is nowhere to go. Give up. Surrender yourself to the darkness."

What could he do? He couldn't possibly fight against that many apparitions, let alone wound them. He thought of the curator's words.

Find yourself. Parallel universe.

He readied himself for suicide, but an unseen force stole the knife from his hands.

"It's not going to be so easy for you, Bobby," said a wraith.

Bob ran through the museum exhibits and caught sight of an instrument of death. "Then I guess I'll have to improvise."

He dashed over to the guillotine, lay his head down, and wrangled the rope. Too late. They were already coming. He scrambled to his feet and rushed to the gallows. No use. And then he moved to the iron maiden, climbed in, and pulled it shut. A wraith reached out but missed. His life slowly left him; the apparition stared on.

"It's only a matter of time. We will find you, and when we do, you will become one . . ." The voice began to fade. "With the . . . darkness . . . with . . . us."

Episode 8: Live, Die, Repeat (Unwillingly)

I KNOW WHAT YOU'RE thinking. "Bob, what the hell is going on here now?"

Well, folks, I ain't so sure myself. Apparently, I'm going Dr. Who every time I ax myself. So, what happens from here on out? I'm not quite sure. Truth be told, I'm scared shitless, and I sure as hell don't wanna 'become one with the darkness.' I'm pretty sure that doesn't mean signing up with the band or being Tim Curry's protégé in *Legend*, either.

I guess . . . I guess this is going to be it.

Bob awoke in his bed. Alone. He heard no one in the house. It was quiet. Abnormally quiet. Typically, it was bustling with the kids running amok and his wife shouting after them. His lips curled into a smile at the thought.

He lay in bed, wondering. Wondering what in the hell was going on. Who was *this* Bob? What kind of life did he lead? Was he a good father? A loving husband? A schmuck?

A has-been? He sighed as he got out of bed and wandered to the mirror above the dresser. He looked his body over. Bullet wounds, stab wounds, rope burns, fire burns. The marks of his suicides were manifesting at an alarming rate. He stared at his reflection hard; he barely recognized himself. Would other people?

He then performed a morning ritual he hadn't completed since his newfound "power" arrived—he had a shower. He shaved, brushed his teeth, clipped his nails. All the things he had almost forgotten about. He stared at himself in the mirror again. The reflection seemed to cry out in agony, pain . . . deceit. A man trapped within. Screaming. Begging. Yearning for freedom. This spurned the sadness within more and invoked those ever-burning feelings that had first started his perpetual-motion self-killing machine. He gazed down at the razor on the sink. He debated with himself.

Don't you ever get tired of it all?

Well, yeah, I am tired. So drained.

Why do you keep running? If what he said is true, then doing anything is pointless.

There's always hope.

Was hope there when you first jumped? When you first started the chain of events that led you to where you are now?

No, but that was my choice. A bad one, sure, but it was still _my_ choice.

And yet, you continue to evade the real thought, the real answer to your question. You know it's pointless. You recognize it's all going to come crashing down on you. You know you're going to lose. And . . . You. Hate. Losing. That's all you've known. You're just one big walking contradiction, talking about "choices and hope." You're pathetic.

If I could take it all back and try again, I would. I would make an effort, and I would better myself. I want to fight.

And with that thought, Bob turned away from the mirror and the razor and exited the bathroom. He stepped with a purpose, something he hadn't felt in a long, long time. He dressed in his best attire and set out for the day.

He wagered that his wife and kids were probably at school and work since it seemed like that typical kind of day. He wandered into the city and ventured downtown. There was no knife, no wraiths, nothing. But as much as he wanted to believe otherwise, he knew it was only a matter of time. He found himself at the bank; a feeling drew him in. He looked around and saw nothing out of the ordinary.

The clock struck noon, and in came a group of men donned in black. They wore masks bearing different presidents' faces and waved automatic guns around, occasionally firing a few rounds in the air. One carried a bag, probably filled with small bombs or plastic explosives, Bob assumed. Everyone got down on the ground except for him. He wasn't afraid of death. And he surely wasn't scared of them.

"Get the fuck down on the ground, you piece of shit!" shouted a man in a Ronald Reagan mask.

He clubbed Bob over the head and kicked him when he was on the ground. "Don't even fucking think about trying to be a hero!"

The other men in masks—the faces of Lincoln, Clinton, G. W. Bush, Nixon, Obama, and Donald Trump—jumped over the counter as an armored truck burst through the front entrance. More men in masks jumped out and began tying up hostages while taking their phones, wallets, jewelry—anything of value.

Reagan-mask came back to Bob. "Alright, dickhead, let's see what you got." Bob lay there calmly, though he could feel the rage beginning to swell inside. He watched the criminals hit women, some with their kids. They told them they would be taken, raped, and then killed. That no one would find their bodies and that their kids would be sold into slavery and human trafficking. Bob had had enough.

"You're pathetic," said Bob to Reagan-mask.

"What was that, fucker?"

Bob sat up and stared deep into the man's eyes. "I said, you are a fucking coward. All of you."

Reagan-mask laughed. "Oh yeah? I got the gun, *bitch.*" He colt-copped Bob with his gun and sent him back to the floor. "You're gonna wish you never opened your mouth, man. I'll fucking end your life, then your family's."

Bob started to laugh. All eyes were on him.

"You don't even know what I've been through, what I've seen. You—all of you are lower than the pieces of shit that I flushed down the toilet this morning. You are *nothing.* Nothing but cowards who hide behind masks, scared of reality, scared of being caught, scared—terrified of all of us, having to use guns. You're weak. Pathetic."

He spat blood on the floor.

"Oh yeah? Who's gonna save ya, pal? No one. And there ain't a God damn thing you can do about it," said Reagan-mask with a grin.

Bob grinned back. Maniacally. "No, *friend*, you're wrong. I'm gonna kill you, all of you. I will see to it that you're all gutted and left to rot on this floor. These people will be freed by my hands."

Reagan-mask lifted his gun to shoot Bob in the head.

That's when it happened.

58

Bob drew the knife from nothingness and slit Reagan-mask's heels and drove the blade into his chest. Two shots rang out. The rest of the gunmen raised their arms.

Bob rolled to his feet and dashed towards the next masked man. He slit Bush-mask's throat and let him take a few bullets while moving on. Next targets: Lincoln-mask and Nixon-mask. They killed each other when Bob got between them. He stole a handgun and returned a few shots as he ran at the masked men by the truck. They dropped. Then, it was over the counter after the Obama-mask. He dove and snapped the man's neck like a twig as he grabbed the bag slung around it.

The feeling, the rush, the excitement—it was nothing like anything he'd ever experienced. He thirsted for blood but not for the blood of innocence as he once had. He looked around. Most of the remaining men had climbed into the armored truck and attempted to flee. They were of no concern to Bob now. Police had descended on the scene and fired wildly at the vehicle. The only one left in the building was the man in the Trump mask, who had taken a woman and child hostage, a knife to the boy's throat, and a gun pointed at the mother's head.

"Don't even fucking think about it, bud," said Trump-mask. "You don't even know what you've gotten yourself into!"

Bob slowly walked towards him. "I think you have it all wrong. You don't even know what *you've* gotten yourself into. You know you're about to die, one way or another. Yet, you would jeopardize this woman and child to save yourself? Sad."

"Don't come any closer! I'll fucking do it!"

Bob shrugged. "Two lives to save thirty or forty? Those are odds I can live with."

Police shouted over the loudspeaker, ordering the man to stand down: "You're completely surrounded. Don't be stupid."

"Hear that?" asked Bob.

"Who the fuck are you?" The masked man had fear in his voice now.

"Just another guy who's tired of being wronged by assholes like you."

The man motioned to slit the boy's throat and pull the trigger. Time slowed down. Bob noticed and took advantage of this. He moved his knife up to the man's throat and raised his gun to his head while pulling the boy and woman away, dislocating their shoulders with the jerking force. As time resumed its usual speed, Bob grinned.

A bang and a sudden gasp for air. The man lay crumpled on the floor in a bloody mess. The mother and child cried out in shock.

Police advanced. They had pulled some men out of the armored truck alive. *Shame*, Bob thought.

The knife disappeared, and Bob fell to the floor. Blood poured out from underneath him onto the cold marble tile. Life didn't leave him. He fought this time, trying to keep hold of what mattered the most to him.

"Show me your hands!" an officer shouted as he approached.

Bob slowly raised his hands above his head, legs sprawled. The darkness was coming.

"He saved us!" some people cried out.

The last thing Bob heard before passing out was the police calling out for medical personnel, and the last thing he thought was . . .

Being the hero for once was nice.

Episode 9: All Bets Are Off

Part One

"YOU'RE LUCKY TO BE alive, bud."

The voice seemed close, male. Probably one of the cops.

"I have to say, I'm impressed by your prowess. I haven't seen anyone do that before, let alone go out of his way to help others as much as you did."

There was a slight chuckle. Bob's eyes darted around, but still, he saw only darkness.

"Shame, though, all that effort just to wind up in a prison for the sick. You're one step closer, ya know? To death."

This . . . This wasn't a cop, a doctor, or anyone he knew. Who the hell was it?

"You see, Bob, I've been watching you for a while now. I've watched your descent into madness, your struggle, your highs, your lows—everything. Now, you're just caught in the whirlwind of a never-ending war you don't know about or care to know about. Ah, I suppose ignorance is bliss. A luxury that many of us are not familiar with and cannot afford." The voice sighed. "But I guess . . ." It seemed to move around him before continuing. "Life itself is a never-ending war between emotions, right and wrong, poor and wealthy, and so on. Such a long list of atrocities we can invent."

There was a long pause. The voice seemed to be observing Bob. Or something.

"You will eventually face your end, Bob, and when you do, you'll have to make a choice. Things are going to get harder. Those you love will die. You will be betrayed. You will be tested beyond what you have come to know. Think about the endgame, not the here and now."

He heard a short series of footsteps. The voice was leaving. "Do try to keep this in mind, will you?"

Sometime later, Bob awoke. Machines beeped and took his vitals. He looked down at the IV in his hand. The scars still showed themselves to him, but clearly, they were invisible to others. He thought back on the man who'd visited him. Who was he? What part did he play?

A female doctor entered the room, clipboard in hand. "Ah, it's good to see you're awake. I have to inform you about some bad news, though."

Bob furrowed his brow in confusion. "What?"

The doctor looked down at the clipboard and then at him. "You have an advanced form of cancer. Something we don't even know about. It's attacking your body aggressively and moving fast. I . . ." She paused. "I can't even give you a proper timeline." The doctor wiped her brow. "I suggest that you get your affairs in order."

Bob stared blankly at her. "I have cancer?" Then he chuckled. "That has to be the most asinine thing I've heard in a while."

"I understand it's hard to take in," said the doctor.

Then, a male police officer entered the room and knocked on the open door. "Excuse me."

"Oh, officer, can I help you?" asked the doctor.

"I need to have a moment with him if you don't mind."

The doctor nodded and left the room, closing the door behind her.

Bob stared at the man. What now?

"I'm afraid I have some bad news for you," the officer began. "There is no easy way to tell you this, but . . ."

Bob's stomach filled with agonizing despair, which increased a hundredfold when the officer continued.

"Your family was . . ."

No . . .

". . . in an accident."

No—no, please, God, no.

"No one . . ."

Don't you fuckin' dare say it!

". . . survived."

Bob stared. Felt his heart rate elevate. Blood pressure—high. The machines cried with Bob as tears flowed.

"I am so sorry for your loss," said the officer apologetically, his cap in hand.

"How?" Bob asked. "How did they die?"

The officer gathered himself before telling him that someone shot them while they were stopped at a red light. They suspected the action was gang-related, but they couldn't verify it.

Bob tried to regain control, gritting his teeth and clenching his fists. "Do you have any leads? Suspects?"

"Just a general description that fits most of those in the gang that walks the streets around here."

"Thank you," said Bob, as he tried to hold back more tears. And rage.

The officer nodded and left the room.

There Bob sat, alone, with all the worst news ever to be conceived.

Nothing. I have nothing left that matters to me.

The thought of suicide seemed delightful to Bob. However, he had something more in mind.

Part Two

Bob sits on the edge of his hospital bed. He has been discharged. His wounds are healed enough.

I gotta tell ya, folks, there really isn't a rhyme or reason for me to stay alive anymore. The kids, my wife, they're gone. They're dead. All dead. I—I just don't know.

Bob cries.

I can't believe it, and I don't want to believe it, but when I saw their lifeless bodies at the morgue . . .

Bob grits his teeth and rocks back and forth, clenching his fists, struggling to maintain composure as the vivid and horrible pictures flash on the backs of his eyelids.

Those sons of bitches! I'm gonna make them pay. I'm gonna make them wish they were never fucking born, that they'd never messed with my family or with me!

Bob looks down at a picture of himself with his wife and kids. Tears stain the photograph and the handgun.

"C'mon, man!" the gang member pleaded as he stared at the pistol barrel between his eyes. "I don't know anything about no kids or woman! Just let me go!"

"No, no. Don't you dare fucking play that shit with me. You and your boys murdered my family in cold fucking blood." Bob pistol-whipped the man across the jaw, then grabbed him by his mangy hair. "Now, you're gonna tell me *who* and where they all are. If you do that, then I won't end your pathetic life right here, right now."

"I don't know, man," he cried. "I don't know what you're talking about. I just got into the gang last week. I don't even know where they meet up. It's always changing."

Bob knew he was honest; honesty was rare in a street thug. "Let me tell you something. You get outta here. You don't *ever*, ever think about doing something like this or being a part of some gang, ya hear me? If you do, if you fucking think about it, I will find you and kill you. It doesn't even matter if you think I'm lying—I will find you, and I will fucking kill you. Got it?"

The man nodded as snot and tears streamed down his face. He scurried off into the streets, eventually out of sight.

Bob caught the eye of a witness and decided to give chase. He figured someone had been tailing the newbie, ensuring he wouldn't foul up. Now, he'd return to the rat's nest to tell all the rats about what had happened. Bob counted on it.

He was eventually led to a seemingly abandoned apartment building. The odds of surviving the encounter were slim, but he didn't care. Death wasn't as threatening as what the wraiths had promised.

Meandering through the hallways and peering into each room, Bob took note of the gang's residence. *They're here, alright.*

He came at last to the top floor.

"You got a lot of balls for coming here, old man," a man yelled.

"You assholes killed my wife and my kids," said Bob calmly. "So now I'm here for your lives."

Gang members filed out from every room, surrounding Bob. They all clenched various weapons. Some had masks on, while on others, he could see sadistic grins. "You ain't getting them, buddy. You're dead meat."

Bob could feel the anger swell up within. "Death offers no comfort for me. I pray it holds torment for you, just as much as you've caused for me."

The gang's leader stepped forward, a young man in a skull mask, donning all black. "I could kill you where you stand. Your life belongs to me now. You know that, right?"

Bob closed his eyes. He envisioned how the forthcoming events would play out. "I belong to no one and no god."

"Kill him," said the leader with a sly smile.

Part Three

The thugs came at Bob one by one at first, like morons. One swung a baseball bat wildly. Bob punched him in the throat with all his might, and the man dropped to the ground instantly. Then they came in droves. Bob couldn't help but smile at the thought of the overwhelming odds.

They had machetes, hammers, crowbars, baseball bats, cattle prods, and God knows what else. Those with guns were told to hold that the leader wanted to see the folly of the fool who had come to meet his death.

Bob took a few hits here and there but always returned the thugs' offering tenfold. "You call that a knife?" he said as one displayed his fancy knife skills. Bob unsheathed the dagger of darkness. "Here's a knife." The blade glowed red, emanating the hatred and anger flowing within Bob. All the thugs laughed and advanced.

Bob hacked and slashed his way forward, occasionally getting hit, cut, or knocked down to the ground. He'd just get back up, the fire within fueling his rage. Images of his dead family nearly caused him to lose all control. He couldn't let that happen.

The thugs' numbers were starting to dwindle. Finally, the gang leader had had enough. He gave the signal: annihilate by gunfire.

Bob laughed hysterically before collapsing on the ground. "You think you can hide behind your pathetic weapons and goons? It doesn't matter if I die here—I will come back, I will find you, and I will kill you. I will make it as slow and painful as possible."

The leader grinned smugly. "Look at you, old man. You're done. You brought this on yourself. Now you can join your whore and brats in death."

Bob coughed. "Thanks, kid. That's just what I needed."

Gunfire rained down on him. Bullets whizzed and ricocheted off walls. Time slowed down again, much like it had in the bank. Bob gathered his rage, his vengeance. And then exploded forward.

He slit throats, stabbed evil hearts, drove the blade of vengeance through wicked skulls. The blood feast fueled the dagger, increasing Bob's speed, power, and anger. As he approached the last few shooters and the leader, he started to see the red haze. He was blacking out. A few bullets had hit him, but it was nothing of substantial concern. He focused on the pain, using it to root himself in reality. He decapitated the shooter to the left of the leader, then stabbed the other multiple times in the gut before using them both as a shield and shooting the rest with their guns. Lastly, he tossed the man over the rail for good measure.

Time became present once more, active, unwavering. Here, Bob stared into the eyes of the gang leader. Cold, lifeless eyes. A doll's eyes. He smirked. He wondered what his eyes looked like right now.

The leader disappeared from Bob's gaze to look at the carnage that had befallen his gang. "What . . . what the hell happened!"

"I told you I would save you for last and make your death as painful as possible. I aim to keep that promise."

"Look, man, c'mon, you can't be serious!" pleaded the thug leader. "I—I got a wife and kids too, I got a sick mom. I just—"

"JUST WHAT!" Bob roared. "I had a wife and kids, too—and you took them from me!" He moved a step closer to the man before him. "You think I will show you pity? Mercy? No, I have none to offer someone like you."

"C'mon, man!" The thug faked a punch and then pulled his ace, shooting the vigilante in the chest. "That's what you get, bitch!"

Bob tumbled to the ground, bleeding profusely. The man stood over him with the gun pointed straight at his face. "Where's your talk now, bitch? You ain't nothing!"

Bob smirked as he coughed up some blood. "I had planned this from the start."

The thug cried out as his Achilles tendons were severed. "I will die, yes," said Bob calmly. "But everyone dies. I will go to the dark after you do. However, I will not stay dead. I can't say for sure if you will." Bob rolled over and started to slice more tendons and make small cuts all over the thug's body. "If you do, though, I suggest you give up your life of crime, disband your gang, help others, spend time with your alleged wife and kids, and help your mother." He gripped the man's skull firmly before slicing off his ears, nose, and eyelids. "You never know when you're going to go. You should make the most of life." He then cut out the man's tongue and forced it down his throat.

Bob sat back as the thug choked on his blood and tongue. "I could have done worse. Not my best work, though. Then again, I was always killing myself, never really others. Still . . . it's something to be admired."

The man gagged and died soon after.

Bob lazily got to his feet and wandered to the rail. He could feel life leaving him again, a familiar sensation. He heard a howling sound. Was it the wind? Or something else?

Red and yellow eyes began to pierce the veil; he knew them well. The wraiths were coming for him again. Perhaps he owed that thug a favor in a sense—he needed to leave *this* world. But the kids . . . his wife.

One day, we'll be together. I hope.

He shed tears for his family as the wraiths drew near, their arms outstretched, ready to take him.

"Sorry, boys, not today," he said, willing the knife deep into his heart.

As darkness crept in, Bob thought, perhaps they'd spared him after all—while the souls of the gang screamed, shredded in the dark by something far worse.

Episode 10: Sweating Out My Sins

Part One

BOB AWOKE ATOP A building that was being built. Startled, he wrapped his legs tight around a steel beam. "How the fuck did I get up here?"

He looked around; a rope had been tied around the beam. It ended in a noose, which was around his neck. Apparently, his parallel self had wanted to make a grand gesture. The city sprawled out in magnificence that stretched for miles upon miles. He looked towards the direction of his home, nestled beneath the trees, past the river.

In his pocket was a yellowed, worn book that resembled a journal, perhaps from an older Bob. He thumbed through some of the pages before it slipped from his fingers and fell to the sidewalk below. He supposed that Bob had tried in vain.

Then he remembered.

Visions of his family—dead, cold, lifeless. He brought his hand up, feeling the noose and some of the scars around his neck. They were still manifesting slowly. What reason did he have to exist anymore? If his family was gone and he had exacted vengeance, why stay in the world? Perhaps he should let the wraiths come and get him. Give up. Call it quits.

He thought of his family and friends. His old life. Good times. Better times. It was all behind him now.

Slowly, he shifted his weight and slid off the beam. He fell fast before the rope reached maximum tension, and his neck snapped like a twig. It was one of his quickest deaths. One of the smoothest. As he left this world—this universe—he watched his body sway in the wind. A pendulum with no direction, no purpose. For there was no time that remained for him to tell.

Bob awoke again, this time at home, in his bed. He lay on his back and stared at the ceiling. Depression set in, hurling him deeper into the abyss. He eventually sat up, planted his feet on the floor, and buried his head in his hands. He wept until autopilot switched on, and then he strolled around the home that was nearly absent of life, save for him. He thought of the laughter of children, his children, and the sound of his wife announcing dinner time. The sun peered through the kitchen, illuminating where they had sat for their meals.

Absence.

Lifeless.

The emptiness within him grew.

Bob noticed a piece of paper sticking out from his wallet on the kitchen island. He reached for it and opened it up. Sitting on the floor, he read slowly, absorbing the words left by his late wife, and wept.

After a while, Bob got to his feet, tucked the paper in his wallet, and took it and his keys out to the garage, along with a rag, which he stuck in one of the gas cans. After lighting it, he backed the car out and sat in the street, watching the flames consume the garage and the rest of the house. He closed his eyes briefly and set off. Anywhere but here.

As he drove away, the flames took on the silhouettes of his wife and kids. They waved goodbye and then vanished.

Honey,

I want you to know that if I ever go before you, that if anything happens to me . . . I love you. I always have, and no matter what, I always will. I will be with you, by your side. There is no other person I could ever see myself with. I feel like we've always been together, and, well, I think that even when it is our time, we will be together in death. At least, that's a hope I'd like to have.

Whenever I look at our kids, I see us. I see the best of times and the worst of times. I see all that we've strived to be and what we are capable of. I know you have your good days and your bad days. I know you struggle with your emotions and are afraid to speak of them. Talk to me about all the pain you go through. I know it's difficult for you to open up and that you feel you must take on the burden of everyone's weight to be the hero.

Society warps our minds and programs us to be people we aren't. It's a shame, that awful stigma, that one is weak if he feels he can't handle a burden alone. You need not carry the weight alone. When we married, it was "in sickness and health" through the good and the bad. You're not alone, sweetheart.

I want you to know that I know things will be hard. You have to be strong, though. Not just for the kids but for yourself, too. So, don't let the dark days take over. Remember that I love you, as do the kids. And I guess your friends, too. I suppose they can count.

I love you, always and forever.
Jill

Honey,

I want you to know that if I ever go before you, that if anything happens to me . . . I love you. I always have, and no matter what, I always will. I will be with you, by your side. There is no other person I could ever see myself with. I feel like we've always been together, and, well, I think that even when it is our time, we will be together in death. At least, that's a hope I'd like to have.

Whenever I look at our kids, I see us. I see the best of times and the worst of times. I see all that we've strived to be and what we are capable of. I know you have your good days and your bad days. I know you struggle with your emotions and are afraid to speak of them. Talk to me about all the pain you go through. I know it's difficult for you to open up and that you feel you must take on the burden of everyone's weight to be the hero.

Society warps our minds and programs us to be people we aren't. It's a shame, that awful stigma, that one is weak if he feels he can't handle a burden alone. You need not carry the weight alone. When we married, it was "in sickness and in health" through the good and the bad. You're not alone, sweetheart.

I want you to know that I know things will be hard. You have to be strong, though. Not just for the kids but for yourself, too. So, don't let the dark days take over. Remember that I love you, as do the kids. And I guess your friends, too. I suppose they can count.

I love you, always and forever.

Jill

Part Two

BOB DROVE AROUND THE city for a while, thinking. His cell phone had been continuously ringing since he left the house. No doubt it was relatives trying to reach him. Probably hoping he'd finally killed himself, and they were left with the remaining inheritance and payouts. *Vultures*, he thought.

He parked at his new hangout, his place of solitude, since most of the guys at work—and some of his friends—never bothered with him. It was his gateway to forgetfulness, and he needed it now more than ever. This particular bar had come to help him battle his depression, which was contradictory, he knew. But his alcoholism wasn't a result of depression—it was just how his family was. "Luck of the Irish," he supposed.

He pulled up a chair at the rail and sank his heavy head.

"What'll it be?" asked the bartender.

She was cute, the kind you could get to know. The kind you could do a lot of dirty things to. That was the last thing on his mind, but still, he smiled. "Two shots of house vodka, please."

Two full shot glasses appeared, and in an instant, they were gone. Bob signaled for two more.

"Rough day," she asked.

"You could say that."

"Well, let me know if there's anything I can help you with, hon," she said, pouring him two more shots. Then, like the wind, she was gone, walking away to help other patrons.

Out of hardwired habit, he checked her out. Smirking, he shook his head.

Out of the corner of his eye, he saw a few unsavory folks. Some he knew well enough by their conversations. He'd never intentionally listen in, but whenever he overheard talk about raping women, molesting kids, and luring unsuspecting folks, he came to give a damn. He'd given anonymous tips to the police but figured some of these folks had connections. Quite a few were dressed in flashy suits. It was like the Rapists of the Round Table. The only thing missing was some poor sap bound and gagged in the middle. And a gangbanging.

Bob had had about enough of all the kiddie talk they were having. Of course, nowadays, he didn't give a rat's ass if they noticed him or not. He had a new way of life. A new way to discipline folks. Justice to serve to those he deemed wicked. He would be the voice of those hurt and those silent. *Soon*, he thought. *Soon the world is going to be a whole lot brighter without you, sick fucks.*

He signaled the bartender. While he waited for his drinks, he went over to the jukebox in the corner, near the pedophiles and rapists. They cheered and toasted, having a grand old time recounting their latest despicable acts. He cringed as he made his musical selection. A few took note of him and looked him over. He felt as if he were being mentally killed, groped, or fucked. His stomach turned in disgust. Or maybe it was the vodka on an empty stomach?

One by one, he chose a few songs to set his mood and create an atmosphere. The prelude to murder. He returned to his seat at the bar. Slammed two shots, then three. He was getting dizzy and fast. He motioned the bartender over one last time and ordered another shot of vodka.

"Are you sure, hon? You look like you're about to pass out."

"Don't worry about me, sugar." He smiled.

She came back with his drink.

"Thanks, darling." He raised the mug to her and pulled out all the cash in his wallet. He called her back over. "Here you are, sweetheart. You've been great."

She smiled. "Aw, well, thanks! I hope your day gets better, hon."

Bob shook his head. "Nah, it won't. There's work to be done." The Animals' "House of the Rising Sun" began playing. "I suggest, though, you get somewhere safe. Things are about to get ugly."

As Bob took his knife out, her eyes filled with horror, and she fled for the back room. He headed for the round table of sickos.

"Who the fuck are you? We're busy here!" cried one of the bastards, shooing Bob away.

"You've done enough raping women and kids," Bob said calmly. "Now, you're all about to get fucked by death!"

Blood sprayed their faces, their clothes, and their food as Bob slit the throat of a rather large man. All eyes widened in terror, and the others at the table scrambled in a retaliatory effort. Bob quashed it quick. He did unto them what they had done unto others in four minutes. He overpowered them, stabbing them in the gut, in the groin, in the ass.

Some people stayed to watch it, and some filmed it. Bob cleaned the blade using the tie of one of the wealthier men. Many of them wore wedding rings, he'd noted. His anger only grew.

He walked back to his seat at the bar and stared at the mirror on the wall in front of him. Looking back was a bloody demon of a man. He raised his glass of vodka and drank.

Behind him, police officers began swarming the place. "I waited long enough," he said.

He could feel the wraiths coming for him. "Not today, not tomorrow. I am a slave to no one." Bob raised his knife.

"WEAPON!" an officer shouted. Others shouted orders for him to drop it.

The wraiths came through the walls, one by one. They all stared at Bob inquisitively. Then, a strange thing happened. They gathered up the souls of the pedophiles, molesters, and rapists and dragged them away, kicking and screaming. There remained one.

"Are you waiting for me?" Bob asked.

"It seems . . . we've reached an understanding," it said.

Bob couldn't tell if the being was grinning or what. He had a sense that it was.

Slowly, Bob lowered the knife back into its sheath. "Sorry, boys, I guess I am needed after all." He slowed down time and walked out of the bar into the night to the sounds of Interpol's "Pace is the Trick."

Part Three

It had been a few days since Bob last saw the wraiths. He wandered the city, slaying any he caught doing any of the more heinous human acts. The bodies were piling up, and he was now a wanted man. The thing was—even though he'd get caught in the act of dispensing justice, he could slip away unscathed. Leave the law enforcement officers scratching their heads.

The general public revered him as a hero. But Bob wasn't the man they deserved or needed, nor was he correct in the assumption that he was the bringer of justice. He'd taken that upon himself.

He didn't eat; he didn't sleep. He only wandered alone. He was always cold. He experienced a sort of warmth only when he enacted justice. He felt split, fractured, torn; he was lost. He assumed this was his purpose. However, deep down, Bob suspected it was the blade telling him to do these things, telling him that instead of a vicious murderer, he was a vigilante cleaning up the streets, sort of a modern superhero—some miracle man.

Bob perched on a church roof overlooking the streets below. No cape or cowl, no gadgets, no flight capabilities. Just a man with a bloodthirst and grand illusion—or was it perhaps a delusion? Whatever it was, he knew that eventually, time would catch up with him, along with death. And the wraiths. That day, however, would not be today.

He closed his eyes and listened to the sounds of the city. "Sniffing" the air, he sought evildoers. Then, a great urge sent him reeling over the roof. He flailed about and watched the pavement grow closer every millisecond.

Why? He thought. What could have given him such an urge to jump? Then it hit him. Hard. The sidewalk broke his fall, along with the fire hydrant. Water gushed into the air and overflowed onto the street.

People stopped and looked. He stood up, looking like he had been through Hell and back. His scars were no longer superficial and only visible to him. Everyone saw him. He had lived—he had survived the fall, like a misunderstood angel cast out of Heaven.

Bob felt sick. His stomach turned as he looked at the people of the city. He saw stares of disgust and judgment from those he had wanted to protect and ensure justice for. They had all turned their backs on him.

One by one, they threw stones and debris at him. He covered his face and pleaded with them to stop.

"Monster!" they cried.

"Fiend!" they shouted.

Bob felt warm tears stream down his cheeks. He'd never asked for this, any of it. Tried to make light of a bad situation, and now it was backfiring on him. He felt the anger swell up, all the hatred. Everything he'd once felt before it returned.

"I could kill you all where you stand. After all I've done, you thank me like this? To Hell with you!" He turned and walked away into the church.

Bob was no longer the people's protector and the harbinger of justice. He was simply a man and a broken one at that.

Episode 11: A Helping Hand (Straight to Hell)

Bob moved towards the front-row pew. Candles flickered in the darkened expanse. He wasn't sure if the effect was foreboding or soothing. He took a seat and dropped his head in his hands.

"What troubles you, my son?" asked a man's voice.

He looked up to see an old priest smiling before him. He was blind.

"You . . . can see me?" Bob replied.

"Sight isn't needed to see a troubled soul or feel its anguish," said the priest. "Tell me, what cripples you?"

Bob sighed. "You wouldn't believe me even if I told you, Father."

The priest smiled. "My child, it is not my place to judge you, for our Heavenly Father decides upon that." The man sat next to Bob and put a hand on his shoulder. "Tell your tale, my son. My ears are yours."

Bob nodded. Emotions came and went as he recounted each suicide, each life that was taken. Each battle won . . . lost. The lives that were stolen and forever lost.

"Your anguish is fascinating, I must say," the priest said when Bob finally finished speaking. "I have never heard a tale quite like yours, even in the scriptures. However, you have learned from your mistakes, yes? If given the circumstances, you would change your path?"

Bob thought on this for a moment and then nodded. "Yes, I would've sought help and done more for myself and my family."

The priest nodded. "As they often say, hindsight is twenty-twenty. You don't need eyes to see or know that. The choices we make, though, help shape us into the beings we are. Most think that Heaven is a paradise and that Hell is an eternal prison for the damned. They sometimes forget about Purgatory, depending on the denomination of Christianity. Reflect on blacksmiths and how they forge their weapons. People associate fire with Hell because of what is written in the Testaments. But fire also purifies. Water then soothes and cleanses, restoring us. The air calms us and further soothes us. The mallet helps us, shapes us, and defines us. The mallet is life, and we, well, we are the weapon. We get along when we rest on the rack: peaceful, tranquil, albeit getting dusty. That is with age. However, war drives us to clash, bringing about scratches, dents, and disfigurements. It shatters some and breaks others. Ultimately, we are all gathered up, melted down, reforged, and made anew."

Bob chuckled. "Forgive me, Father, I've just never met quite such an open person of the cloth."

The man smiled. "My son, we of the cloth are not perfect. The ideologies we inflict upon others and our suggestions that there must be one supreme being are just fiction. Faith is the test and testament of what one wants to believe. It is lifelong courage that will bring comfort and solace to those who face mortality and the grave. That is enough if you can ease their pain when their dark hour comes. At least, in my opinion."

"Perhaps you should have gone into politics, Father," Bob said, chuckling again.

"Ah, now there is a subject sensitive to me, my son. I gave up on that 'profession' long ago before my eyes gave out; perhaps that was where they did." The man grinned. "Forgive me, for I must take my leave."

Bob nodded and watched as the priest left, leaving him alone in the church. He felt better. However, he had a nagging feeling in his gut that he couldn't quite explain.

A familiar foreboding voice came from behind him. "Old people. They're such amusing creatures, are they not?"

Bob turned around in the pew and saw a man dressed in black with a red glove on his right hand.

EPISODE 12: THE ART OF ALMOST DYING

BOB STUDIED THE MAN, trying to place him. "I know you. I've heard you before . . . When I was in the hospital? Wasn't it?"

The pale man in black adjusted his red glove and smiled. "Ah, you are remarkable at remembering, aren't you?" He grinned. The man paced around Bob before settling down beside him on the pew. "Yes, I was there. I saw how you cried, the pain you felt, and the sadness within you. Your tormented soul cried for a long, long time, Robert."

"I haven't gone by that name in a long time, *friend*, nor do I intend to now," Bob interjected sharply.

The man put his hands up. "My sincerest apologies . . . *Bob*. I meant no disrespect." The man took in a deep breath and exhaled. "You know, what you've done, the kinds of atrocities you've committed, ordinary folks view that sort of thing as something only a monster would do. And if the religious zealots were to find out that a man is transcending death by killing his parallel-universe selves—do you know what they would do to the likes of you?"

Bob shook his head. "No, nor do I care." He dropped his head in his hands. "I don't care anymore. The priest has given me a bit of closure. If I were to become something more than just a man . . ."

"My friend, man cannot become an angel, at least not in the traditional Christian sense. Nor can they become a harbinger of justice. You're simply a vigilante. No better and no worse than comic superheroes—minus the cape and cowl, of course," said the Man with the Red Right Hand. "However, I can point you in the direction you desperately seek."

Bob picked his head up and looked at the man. "What do you mean?"

Standing, the man began pacing again. "What if I told you that you could get your family back, make all of this disappear? Live your life once again? No consequences."

"I'd think that you're lying and call bullshit."

The man smiled. "Well, I can tell you for certain I'm not bullshitting you . . . Bob."

Bob thought about this. Wanting to jump at a chance at his old life instantly. Still, something seemed off. He figured, though, that he had nothing to lose now. "OK, so then what would I have to do?"

"First things first—let me show you something." With a flick of his right hand, a portal to another plane revealed itself. Bob found himself viewing the world he was familiar with: his home. He saw his wife and kids, alive, living—without him. He could see the mask his wife wore and the quiet moments she cried alone. A vacant bedside. A broken heart. He lay down on the bed next to her and caressed her face, only to watch his hand pass through her. Tears streamed down his face.

"This is where you formerly existed," said the man. "This is your original timeline—if you will." Another reality appeared. Bob watched the slaying of his wife and kids, and he roared in anger on the streets, only to be seen going to a bar with a revolver and getting drunk. "And this life . . ."

He paused. "This is where you lived, and they died. Do you see the consequences of your actions yet, Bob?"

Bob reached out to touch the bodies of his wife and children, but they slowly disappeared, the sands of their beings dispersing, sifting through his hands. Tears flowed relentlessly, corralled by the growing number of scars on his cheeks.

"How . . . how can I save them?" Bob sobbed, fighting back anger.

"What would you do for your family, Bob? What would you do for those whom you love so much?"

Bob gritted his teeth and snarled. "Anything."

The man grinned. "Then it's quite simple, really. You have to kill an innocent."

Bob's eyes widened. "Wha—what?"

"Take the life of an innocent person. If you do this, you will wake up, in your original timeline, with your wife by your side and your kids sleeping soundly in their beds. Nor will you or they have any recollection of this ever transpiring. You will simply . . . live."

Bob thought of how it would feel to break free of the pain and the torment increasing within. But an innocent person . . .

Taking the lives of those so deserving, in his eyes, those who had it coming and needed to be purged from the world was justice incarnate. If he killed someone innocent, he would be no better than those he had slain or dispensed punishment to.

Finally, he reached a conclusion.

Episode 13: The Joke's on Me

BOB LOOKED AT THE strange man with the red right hand. "Alright, I'll do it."

The man smiled. "I knew you would see reason, Bob. Trust me—you are making the right choice."

Bob nodded. As the two shook hands and departed to the outside world, he saw a pile of priest robes on the floor near the bathroom. His stomach turned a little; knowing.

The outside world roared with city life. People were yelling, cars were honking—it was a home he was becoming accustomed to.

"Now, you will be impervious to any injuries. Mind you, this will go away once your task is finished," said the strange man.

Bob eyed him. "How do you know I won't use that against you?"

"Because I know you, friend. You want to see your family. And I am by no means innocent," the man replied with a grin. "I have a specific target for you. I felt it would be better for you to have an idea and not go into the unknown," he said with assurance. "You are to go to the Artemis Medical Building on Tuesday. Go to the roof at 12:01 p.m. You will then kill the individual with your 'special' knife. And that will be the end of that."

Bob nodded and took in a deep breath.

The Man with the Red Right Hand patted him on the back. "Don't worry, Bob. This is what *you* want. Remember that. Think of what's in it in the end for *you!*"

Bob had made his way to the Artemis Medical Building. It was 11:32 a.m. Tuesday. He looked up to the high roof. He had been here before.

He walked in unnoticed and moved through the halls and stairwells as though he knew the place well.

11:45 a.m.

He got to the roof and waited behind an air conditioning unit, the door in his sight.

11:50 a.m.

He waited and waited for that door to open up.

11:59 a.m.

He remembered then, just like it was yesterday. He opened his wallet, took out his wife's note, and reread it.

12:01 p.m.

The door opened, and a man in a white dress shirt, red tie, black slacks, and black shoes walked out. He walked over to the roof's ledge. Bob caught sounds of sniffling and brief bouts of sobbing.

The stranger's voice with the red right hand echoed in Bob's head. "Go now. Get him before he notices you're there. Push him off the roof. Go back to your time. Go back to your family!"

Bob sighed and cautiously walked over to the man. He heard him light up a cigarette. "Hey, what's wrong, buddy?"

The man wiped his brow, continuing to look out over the city. "I hate it here. I'm worthless. I hate my job. I hate my boss. I hate . . . I just hate my life. All I have are my wife and kids . . . but I think even they hate me."

Bob nodded. "I know what you mean. I used to think I was worthless, that I had no reason to be alive. I wanted to kill myself. I wanted to leave behind my family and this life. I thought they'd be better off without me. I thought that I was so hateful and that life hated me just as much. There was so much anger and rage that had been bottled up. I thought I'd been dealt a shitty hand, and the universe was constantly laughing in my face—no, spitting in it, pissing on me, lighting me on fire, and leaving me to burn."

The man nodded, taking a long drag on his cigarette. "It seems you and I are a lot alike."

Bob walked up to him and put a hand on his shoulder. "More than you know. Then again, we're all in the same boat—more or less."

Bob sighed.

"Then, I lost my wife and kids. I stopped caring and stopped loving myself . . . others. I wanted to die truly. And then a funny thing happened, just when I was at my darkest, just when I thought I couldn't get any lower—I was given a chance to fix it all. All of it." Bob looked around and at the world below. "I realize that I was wrong. I was wrong to believe I could get it all back while taking it away from another. What—no, who gave me that right?" He patted the man on the back. "It'll get better, but only if you work at it. I suggest you take this." He tucked a piece of paper in the man's shirt pocket and walked away.

The man turned to look at his "friend" but found nothing. He opened the paper and began to read, then stepped backward, away from the ledge, sobbing. Taking out his mobile phone, the man called his wife.

"Jill, I—I . . ."

"Bob? Honey? What's wrong?"

"I wanted to tell you that I love you and—and that I need help." Putting his head down in his hands, he sobbed.

The one and only original Bob watched from a distance, smiling. The Man with the Red Right Hand appeared beside him. "Why did you not kill him?"

Bob sighed heavily. "I was wrong. I was wrong to believe that killing someone could change things, bring back my family, solidify my timeline—so you say. That it would make everything better or make the pain go away."

The man smiled and gave Bob a pat on the back. "You've killed yourself countless times. You always gave yourself that little push, and each time, you believed that by killing yourself, you would make life better for your wife and your kids. You believed that your life would be better absent of all things. Now you finally understand yourself."

Bob looked at the man. "What? What do you mean?"

"Come. It's time to go home, Robert."

"What—where am I going?"

Bob was ushered through a portal that led to darkness. There was no light, no sound, nothing. He felt familiarity around him, though. Soon, sight and sound began to return. He awoke in his bed. He quickly checked his person for scars and impressions and found none. Bob caught a glimpse of the Man with the Red Right Hand in the mirror by the window, who winked and waved goodbye as he disappeared like the dust in the wind. The man's voice echoed in his mind. "Don't throw away your second chance, Bob."

His wife came into the bedroom and started to undress. "Were you talking to someone?" she asked.

"No, just talking to myself," he replied, trying to restrain the tears.

The mysterious stranger's voice echoed again in Bob's head as he and his wife lay side by side. "One day, I may call on you for help. I thought it would be better to let you remember what transpired. Enjoy your life and your family, Bob."

That night, Bob got the best sleep he ever had.

Well, there you have it, folks. Now, I have all of these memories of who I was. What I was. What I had done. What I had become. Now, I'm just a man. A man with the opportunity to make things right—with myself and my family. I think I'll start by enjoying this Thanksgiving dinner.

Still, I can't shake the feeling that the stranger will return someday. Hell, I still don't know that guy's name, either. That's alright, though, because I've got all the time in the world.

THE END . . .

Now let me stop you right there.

You thought that was it? That the credits would roll, some sad-yet-uplifting indie song would play, and you'd walk away feeling like you learned something profound?

Nah. Life's not that generous.

There's always one last thing. One last twist. One last shitty post-credits scene that either changes everything . . . or makes you wish you'd left the theater early.

So go on. Turn the page. I dare you.

EPILOGUE

WELL, HERE WE ARE, folks. A happy ending, right? Ha, you'd think that, but your dear old Bob has some news for ya.

Ya see, while I slept soundly that night after coming back and agreeing to a way back, remember the Man With the Red Right Hand saying he'd need me? Yeah . . . about that . . ."

Some years later, the times were harsh on Bob, as was the cancer. It turned out *that* wasn't something he could escape, no matter the timeline. Then came a visit he least expected . . . somewhat.

There he lay, battered, broken, but not yet beaten, in the hospital bed. He did opt to wither away at home, but Bob didn't want to burden his wife with the fast-approaching chance that death would be visiting, plus, he'd become *quite* pungent.

He let a sigh escape that outran the machine's beeps; he looked out to the sunny day that was oblivious to those who suffered, much less cared for those who died—time walks over those bodies left in the dust.

Then . . .

"Hello, Robert."

The familiar voice sent a rush of anger through Bob's languid veins. He turned his head, expecting one visitor but finding another.

"I fucking told you—oh, it's you." Bob saw *him* again, likely making good on his last promise.

"You look like shit," said the Man with the Red Right Hand with a smile.

Bob sighed. "Well, I can't quite say I am surprised to see you." He then let a laugh escape, clenching his sides in pain. "Though I gotta say, I kinda figured you knew this was how it would be for me, huh?"

The Man with the Red Right Hand shrugged. "Fate is an interesting thing; there is no predetermined factor; we're all capable of wielding ways and methods to change it—whether by force, will, coercion, or—" then he smiled, "an offer from an old friend."

Bob felt an icy chill run up and down his body, an uneasiness set in his gut, or maybe it was just the chemo making him feel like he had to shit again.

"You really have a way with words, buddy. I figured you'd come to cash in that promise, and behold, here you are. Right when I'm about to fuckin' die." Bob sighed. "Though, it ain't all been that bad. I had some years from it, got to see my kids grow, and had some success. Shit, did you know I actually got help and had my thoughts under control?"

The Man with the Red Right Hand now stood beside Bob's bedside, smiling. "I know, I've checked in on you occasionally. You've really come a long way, Robert—" he raised his hands, "Sorry, *Bob*."

Bob shook his head. "That's some stalker bullshit right there, sir." He chuckled.

The Man began to pace and then stopped by the window, looking out. "I *am* proud of you, Bob. I didn't think you had it in you at first, but surprises are just that. You really did change for the better, and now, I have come asking for your help in a precious matter for me."

"Why does this sound like a terrible thing is going to happen to me again . . . like I ain't scared of dying, hell, you know that, at least you oughta know," said Bob, with labored breaths.

"Indeed. No, what I am going to ask of you is going to make you wish you could kill yourself all over again, but I also know . . . just how curious you are."

"You have my attention," said Bob.

The Man with the Red Right Hand turned around. "I'd like for you to come work for me. I want you to record human history—a chronicler, watching over the fates that befall humankind and—"

"I'll do it," said Bob, sternly.

"Ah, you didn't let me finish," said the Man with a sly grin. "You should always hear the terms and conditions before agreeing, even with me, my friend."

Bob shook his head. "I know you well enough, and I *do* owe you for what you did for me. So if it's reading and writing for a while, yeah, I can do that. It's not like I'm doing much, let alone where I'll go when I die."

The Man shook his head and sighed. "You're too kind, though your qualities remind me a lot of myself when I was younger and a certain friend of mine; that's probably why I took such a fascination with you. Ah, but I digress. Like your jumping days, your consciousness would likely scatter to the winds of time and space, becoming a 'déjà vue' to your other selves, but nothing would change. You'd just be less than a blip." He leaned in toward Bob. "In the grand scheme of things, it's quite intimidating, isn't it?"

Bob shrugged. "We think we're at the top of the food chain, the champion of apex predators, but we're nothing that special, other than that we have a slightly higher thought process, made a wheel, and love to fight one another."

The Man with the Red Right Hand laughed. "You're quite remarkable, Bob. Even when you're legitimately facing mortality in the face, you still carry on in *your* own way." He straightened himself up. "In a few days, I will come to get you and take you away. The cancer will win, but think of it as a sort of . . . tie-breaker." He gave a wink, and then, in an instant, he was gone.

Bob groaned. "Man, please don't do that again. Especially knowing that you probably have seen me wank." His stomach turned and bubbled and surged with tremendous pain. "Hoo, the nurses are going to be so pissed with me, urgh!"

What followed was an unpleasant sound and aroma, but to Bob, it was a Monday, and he was finally getting his revenge by shitting the bed.

Afterword: Bob's Dream Journal

Filed Under: Shit I Can't Tell My New Therapist Without Getting Measured for a Straitjacket

So yeah, journaling. Apparently, it's the self-help craze du jour, or at least that's what Carol—drowning in her third beige cardigan and the overwhelming scent of lemon pledge—would have me believe.

"Write it all down, Bob," she chirped, like a motivational bird with a Xanax problem. "It'll help you organize your thoughts, identify patterns, track your triggers."

Right. Sounded about as appealing as a root canal. That was before the dreams started morphing from the usual bizarre nighttime nonsense into . . . this.

Now, I'm waking up, chewing my tongue bloody, or nursing bruised knuckles from a satisfyingly violent fistfight with my reflection (who, by the way, is a total bastard). There was also that memorable dream at the pharmacy where a guy popped a few lithium tabs and spontaneously combusted into a glittery mushroom cloud of confetti. You know, the usual.

So, yeah, Carol's little tip? It was not exactly the mental laxative I was hoping for; it was more like a stick of dynamite shoved where the sun doesn't shine, you know, face-down, ass-up kinda deal—and not in the fun way. These aren't just garden-variety bad dreams; they feel like fissures themselves.

I'm writing them down now, not for the supposed benefits of therapy (which is clearly about as effective as a screen door on a submarine). Not for some delusional sense of clarity (ha!). And not because I secretly desire to relive this existential dumpster fire.

No, I'm documenting this descent into madness because a terrifying thought has taken root: these aren't just dreams. They feel like echoes of other timelines, like I'm slipping between realities, catching glimpses of lives I've somehow stumbled into. Sometimes I'm convinced these fractured narratives belong to others I've met. They feel disturbingly familiar at other times, like half-forgotten memories resurfacing in grotesque new forms. Most of the time, the line blurs into oblivion.

In one, I can fly, albeit with the grace of a drunken pigeon plummeting towards earth. Met another flyer in that one, looked like he was born with wings, the smug bastard.

In another, I die trying to protect some poor sap I was initially hired to off—a delightful paradox orchestrated by yours truly.

Sometimes I even manage to die twice in the same damn loop. And then there are the times I'm just *Confused Bystander #3*, with a front-row seat to the apocalypse, popcorn and drink not included.

And when I finally claw my way back to consciousness—sweating, maybe screaming a little, definitely smelling faintly of ozone or bourbon, I swear I didn't touch—the same chilling question always lingers: "Was that a dream I had . . . or one I *was*?"

So yeah, Carol, thanks for that gem of advice. You really cracked me wide open. Turns out, it wasn't enlightenment; it was a goddamn fault line.

Anyway. I decided to call this the "dream journal" mostly because *Scribbled Manifesto from the Mind of a Cosmic Loop Casualty Who Just Wants a Fucking Nap* wouldn't fit on the cover and my handwriting is fucking atrocious. Some of it might make a twisted kind of sense. Most of it won't. But it's here. Every nonsensical, glorious fragment of my not-so-unconscious mind.

What say you and I take a stroll through my nightly existential panic, shall we?

—Bob Barnem

Added this part later.
Different mindset. Different pen. Same old me.
Still can't sleep. Still writing.

—B.B.

So why now? Why keep this going?

Because somewhere along the line, a flicker of something other than dread ignited. Because amidst the recurring deaths and bizarre scenarios, there are still dreams—rare, precious things, like finding a twenty in an old coat pocket—where I don't die. Where I don't fall. Where I wake up . . . and for a fleeting moment, feel almost okay.

And I have this ridiculous, probably delusional hope that maybe, just maybe, if I meticulously document enough of the nightmares, the good ones might start showing up more often. Maybe they'll even . . . stick.

I used to see this journal as some kind of cosmic joke, the universe's way of highlighting my spectacular failure of an existence. But now? Now, it feels . . . different.

Maybe it's just my stubborn refusal to tap out. My small, pathetic way of screaming into the void, "Not yet."

So yeah. Here they are. Most of 'em, anyway.

This is *my* dream journal. Make of it what you will.

—B.B.

Bob's Dream Journal

Breakfast of Existential Champions

MY DREAM LAST NIGHT involved being hunted by a giant, sentient pancake. Its voice—thick, bubbling syrup—shrieked about unpaid breakfast debts and, bizarrely, crimes against wafflekind.

My escape was cut short when I tripped over a sausage link that felt suspiciously alive, leading to my being devoured whole.

In the syrupy aftermath, a waffle delivered a surprisingly poignant eulogy.

I woke with a desperate craving for carbs and a profound unease about the very essence of breakfast.

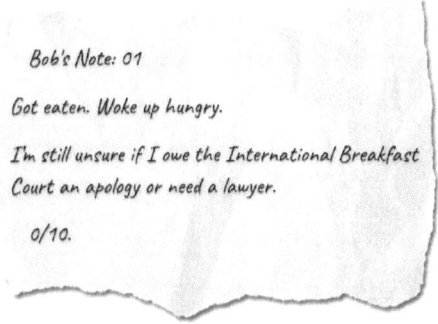

Bob's Note: 01

Got eaten. Woke up hungry.

*I'm still unsure if I owe the International Breakfast
Court an apology or need a lawyer.*

0/10.

The Mirror That Waits

Static buzzed through the featureless gray walls—trapped, restless. It hummed in time with the flicker of the dreadful fluorescent lights.

No door. No window. Only a mirror.

And there was a reflection staring back, but it wasn't mine.

It grinned, all teeth—too sharp, too many—and it kept staring. It didn't mimic me, it just watched.

Then *it* cracked. No, not the glass, but the *image*, fracturing like cheap glass.

But the actual mirror remained untouched. And me? Mostly intact.

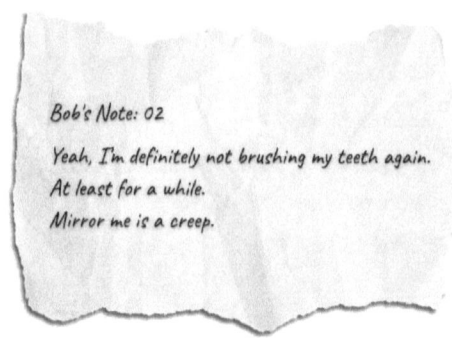

Bob's Note: 02

Yeah, I'm definitely not brushing my teeth again.
At least for a while.
Mirror me is a creep.

The Girl With the Cards

It felt like a rerun that I couldn't turn off. This time, I was definitely in it.

The alley stank of rain and garbage—everything soaked, rotting—like a shitty stew made for yours truly.

The gun felt too real in my hand. Heavy. Final.

Across from me stood a girl who held a well-worn deck of cards. Her calm wasn't soothing, it was surgical, like a knowing glance at the predictable pathetic nature of my current Bob-iteration; like she'd already watched my whole sad story and skipped to the end.

She laid out my fate on the slick grime: Two Aces. Two Eights. A Ten. A Dead Man's Hand. Charmed.

Before I could even react, my hand that gripped the gun erupted—white-hot pain, then nothing.

For a second, my face felt like it was on fire.

She just scooped up her cards, a faint smile her only acknowledgment, and melted into the shadows of the night.

No drama. No flair. Just inevitability.

Bob's Note: 03

Hand: exploded. Face: on fire. Cards: 100% rigged. Pretty sure she cheated, but I guess I probably deserved it.

The Wheel of Utter Misfortune

Bathed in the harsh, desperate glare of game show lights.

The host was a grinning clown whose eyes were empty, burnt-out voids.

The audience was a suffocating sea of my derisive selves.

The Wheel of Fortune spun, each click echoing a lifetime of missteps, the categories a litany of torment: Regret, Panic, Shame, Weaponized Dad Jokes, The Thing I Did Behind the Bleachers in Eighth Grade.

It settled, with cruel irony, on 'Self-Loathing—Daily Double.'

The answer I had to give was myself, as I consumed my tongue. The taste was the bitter tang of failure and the heavy weight of regret.

A hollow roar of canned applause filled the void.

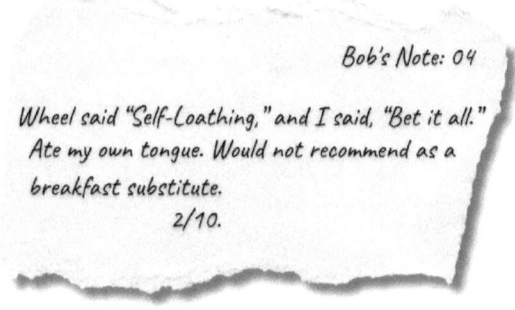

Bob's Note: 04

Wheel said "Self-Loathing," and I said, "Bet it all."
Ate my own tongue. Would not recommend as a
breakfast substitute.
2/10.

The Red Balloon

I try to scream, but my mouth is sealed shut—stitched closed with coarse, dark thread.

An impassive crowd watches as I drown repeatedly in something thick and cold.

The loud crunch of someone eating popcorn cuts through the silence.

In a corner, another figure weeps silently.

A single, cheerful red balloon drifts past my face. It whispers my name in an ancient, cold, and utterly alien voice.

I woke up gasping for air.

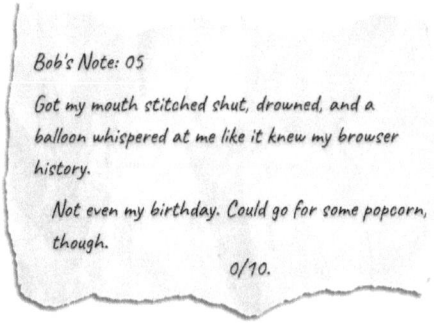

Bob's Note: 05

Got my mouth stitched shut, drowned, and a balloon whispered at me like it knew my browser history.

Not even my birthday. Could go for some popcorn, though.

0/10.

Promotion to Nowhere

The usual rush—late for work, nerves tight—but everything felt hollow.

The office building and my suit were flimsy, painted cardboard on the verge of collapse.

My tie, ha, tightened like a symbolic noose.

Inside my briefcase, sloshed. It was a watery grave for dead, accusing goldfish.

My boss, was a clock-faced figure with time running *backward.*

His words echoed: "Bob, it's time for your exit interview."

Then the floor gave out, and I fell into the buzzing emptiness of static and disappointment.

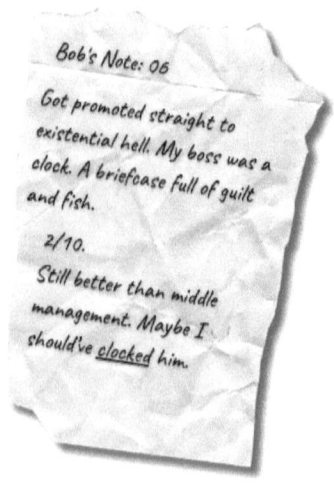

Bob's Note: 06

Got promoted straight to existential hell. My boss was a clock. A briefcase full of guilt and fish.

2/10.

Still better than middle management. Maybe I should've clocked him.

Glitter Bomb at Aisle 5

I was stuck in a pharmacy line, time stretching long enough to contemplate the sweet release of oblivion.

The guy ahead was my mirror image: hollowed out, animated by sheer willpower, caffeine, and possibly generic pain relievers. I think I remembered them saying his name was Harold or something.

Kindred spirit, my brain offered weakly. That was somewhat comforting.

He fumbled in his coat, produced a bottle—looked like my own nightly ritual. He tossed back a few pills like they were candy.

Then—BOOM.

Not a world-ending explosion. More like a joyous, chaotic eruption—an ecstatic birthday party gone feral.

Confetti rained down everywhere. Clouds of shimmering glitter filled the air.

Suddenly, the sterile pharmacy reeked of birthday cake and the faint metallic tang of my own medication.

Panic erupted around me. Screams. People scrambling for safety.

Me? I fucking lost it. I laughed until I couldn't breathe, the kind of laughter that was unrestrained joy that brought tears to my eyes.

Someone cautiously asked, "Are you alright?"

"Nope!" I gasped between peals of laughter. "This is the best goddamn Tuesday I've ever lived!"

If our paths ever cross in the real world, that man deserves a drink. Or maybe just a knowing nod, a silent acknowledgment of the shared, unexpected beauty.

Either way, thank you for the glitter bomb; you're a beautiful disaster.

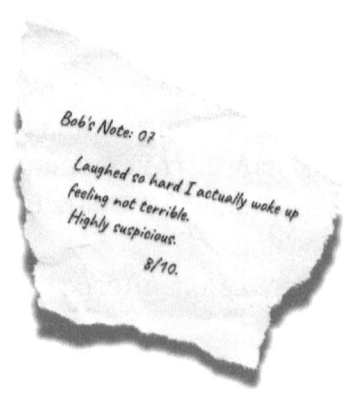

Bob's Note: 07

Laughed so hard I actually woke up feeling not terrible.
Highly suspicious.

8/10.

The Man in the Sky

My usual mode of transport involves a rapid descent—literal or otherwise.

Flying? Not so much.

But there I was, soaring over a reimagined New Boston, skies crowded with grotesque gargoyles clinging to crumbling rooftops.

Somehow, I felt light, weightless, as if I had been copied and pasted from a comic book.

Then I saw him—another figure, just *floating* in the upper atmosphere, miles away, looking down. Now that I think about it, he seemed lost in thought. Well, until he saw me.

His surprise mirrored my own.

We hovered there, separated by distance and the laws of physics, but connected by the sheer absurdity of it all.

A nod. A quiet acknowledgment that, for one impossible breath, we both existed in a place no one should have been.

Then we drifted apart, defying gravity on opposite currents.

Two unlikely souls.

One sky.

No explanation required.

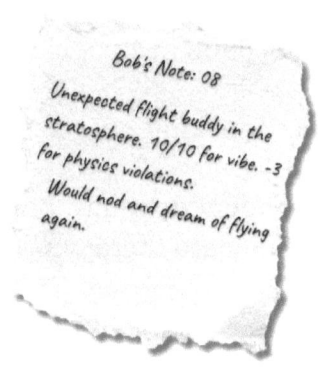

Bob's Note: 08

Unexpected flight buddy in the stratosphere. 10/10 for vibe. -3 for physics violations.

Would nod and dream of flying again.

Crumb Therapy

Back in therapy.

This time, the therapist was a vintage chrome toaster. Yep. Every time I tried to unpack my existential dread, it dinged—*loudly*—and launched a perfectly browned slice of toast squarely at my head.

Wheat, sourdough, white, cheese—which, I did kind of love. Hell, even cinnamon swirl.

Eventually, words failed me, and I resorted to communicating solely through scattered crumbs and profound, nihilistic sighs.

Strangely, this seemed to work.

The toaster nodded, its heating elements glowing like understanding eyes.

"Excellent. We're making real progress," it buzzed contentedly, almost warmly.

Then its slots widened in an apparent attempt to swallow me whole. Standard therapy session, really.

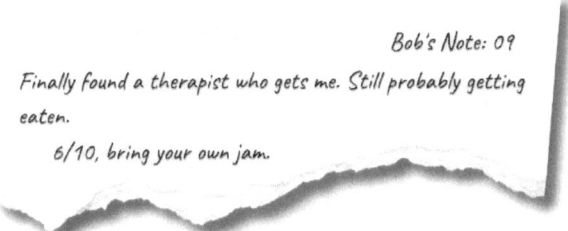

Bob's Note: 09

Finally found a therapist who gets me. Still probably getting eaten.

6/10, bring your own jam.

Steak Knives and Melting Faces

We were all there, around the table.

Grinning. Laughing. That syrupy Norman Rockwell bullshit that rots your teeth.

Then their faces began to melt—softening, sloughing off like wax in a furnace.

The air turned thick with a sickly sweet rot.

The steak knife in my hand suddenly felt less like cutlery, more like a loaded question aimed at my chest.

I wanted to end it—the charade, the loop, maybe *me*.

But I just sat there, mirroring their grotesque, liquefying smiles.

Their screams became background static.

A laugh track in hell.
I woke up soaked in sweat, confusion clinging like static.
And the taste in my mouth? Thick and metallic.
Blood.
I hadn't eaten steak.

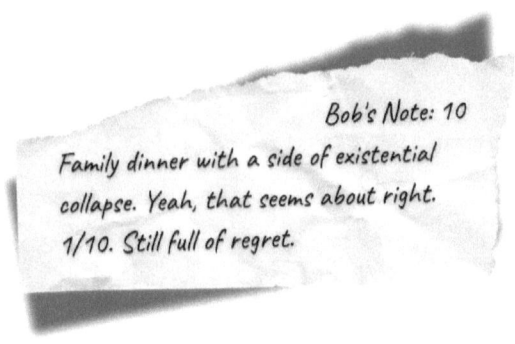

Bob's Note: 10
Family dinner with a side of existential collapse. Yeah, that seems about right. 1/10. Still full of regret.

Highway to Nowhere

I'm driving.

An endless road, a blurring journey. The landscape outside twisted and warped—half-remembered places, half-formed migraines throbbing behind my eyes.

Every exit sign flashed a new way to die: Hanging. Gunshot. Drowning. Self-immolation.

One stark sign read "Marriage," and a bitter thought—*was it really that bad?*—flickered through my mind as my hand twitched on the wheel.

I slammed on the brakes, a futile gesture. The car just laughed, a low mechanical chuckle that vibrated through the cracked leather of the steering wheel, and accelerated into the distorted horizon.

A disembodied voice on the radio droned, "You have reached your destination."

God, I hoped it was wrong.

*Bob's Note: 11   I never liked road trips.
Especially the kind where the GPS only gives you death options.*

Mirror, Mirror, Go to Hell

I was trapped in a maze of reflections. Every wall is a cold, unyielding mirror. And each mirrored Bob looked a little more fractured and broken than the last.

One bore my regrets etched like scars into his skin. Another whispered all the toxic self-recriminations I desperately tried to ignore, his breath cold on my cheek.

They all reached, their eyes hollow voids, their hands icy and slick, like something freshly unearthed. I screamed, a silent tearing in my throat. They smiled, a chorus of my own despair.

I think they were trying to pull me into their mirrored world. Or maybe I was already living there.

Bob's Note: 12
I think I rather have eaten pizza that's pulled out of the crematorium than have this again.

Cliff Notes on Suicide

Standing on the precipice. Jagged rocks clawed at the air below, the wind carrying the faint, salty tang of the unseen ocean. The wind howled, a mournful choir of broken promises.

It felt sickeningly familiar.

The usual script called for a jump. Oblivion. But something held me rooted, my worn boots finding purchase on the gritty texture of the rock.

Hope? Doubt? A glitch in my personal gravity?

Whatever it was, I just stood there. Thinking.

That was the real curse, wasn't it? The endless, agonizing thinking.

Staring into the abyss is overrated. The abyss stares back with a smug little smirk. Bob's Note: 13

The Lodestone Incident

It was a middle-of-nowhere diner screamed 'Nevada' even without a postcard. Lodestone? The milkshakes were legendary. And tonight's entertainment: an alien smackdown.

Spindly gray things dropped from the vents, turning locals into dust with tiny ray guns. Then came the truly brain-scrambling part: they started snapping their spindly fingers in perfect unison. Like some kind of deeply wrong alien flash mob musical. My brain was about to issue an evacuation order when I saw a weird symbol on the greasy menu and jabbed it instinctively.

Bam! Lights down, music up, and Captain E.O. moonwalked his ass out from behind the counter.

He then proceeded to dance-fight the alien invaders into submission. I kid you not. Just when I thought the weirdness had peaked, tentacles shot out from under my booth, wrapped around me like slimy seatbelts, and yanked me through a shimmering hole in reality. Next thing I knew, I was face-to-face with an alien me—antennae and annoyingly flawless skin.

It cocked its head, my voice dripping from its vocal cords, "Ah, Variant7-Sigma. We've been expecting you."

I woke up choking, and the thought of last night's leftovers turned my stomach. Immediate disposal.

Bob's Note: 14

Aliens. Synchronized finger-snapping. Michael Jackson. Nope, definitely not high.

The Door Game

The loop held me fast. Each door I opened was a cruel illusion, returning me to the same scene. Peeling, blood-red wallpaper. A child weeping in the corner, a mirror of past pain. A gleaming knife on a dusty table—potential.

Sometimes, I relived the terror of the child. Other times, I was the wielder, a dark impulse rising within.

The game played on, an endless echo of trauma.

There was no resolution. No winning move. Only the echo of trauma.

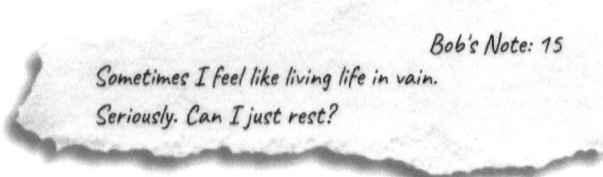

Bob's Note: 15

Sometimes I feel like living life in vain.
Seriously. Can I just rest?

Peace of Mind (Void ~~Where Prohibited~~)

The game show replayed. Or another meticulously crafted torment disguised as entertainment.

The ultimate, unattainable reward? Peace of Mind.

The answers came easily, unbidden—the weight of cosmic dread, the rituals of poltergeist removal, the inherent void of existence.

It was irrelevant.

The clown host, that same recurring bastard, roared with laughter like a damn chainsaw and called every answer wrong.

The laughter resonated deep within—the cruel echo of my own self-deprecation. The 'wrong answer' buzzer was a physical blow, a shotgun blast against my sanity.

This time, the usual chorus of mocking selves remained silent, their silence was worse.

Bob's Note: 16
0/10. Fuck that clown, and fuck the me's, too.

Rats

I dreamed I was a rat.

No, really. Like tail, teeth, twitchy whiskers—*the works.*

I was hanging out in a sewer with a bunch of them, listening to a kid talk to a squirrel. A *Scottish* squirrel. Its name was Red, and a real tough bastard, too.

The kid looked . . . off. Not in a creepy way, like the kind of off you get when someone's been ripped apart and stitched back together wrong, emotionally speaking. Albino, pale as chalk dust, but those eyes? Those eyes had seen some serious shit.

He wasn't scared of Red, the sewer, or even the raccoons watching from the shadows like little murder goblins.

He asked the animals for help. Politely. Like it mattered what they thought. And then they listened. Hell, I listened, and I didn't even know what the hell was going on.

The dream moved around, cutting to scenes like a government black site full of assholes in lab coats talking about "Project Gemini," a handler screaming, "Johnny, respond!" while the kid sobbed in a cage, and he hugged a dog that barked back *actual words.* (I think the chihuahua said, "I'll kill for you." Which . . . yeah. That tracked.)

Then it got weird.

There was a dude named Jerry, who I swear looked like someone I knew once, maybe even me. He tried to help the kid and gave him a place to stay. Then, someone took Jerry away. Like permanently. Unalived him.

The kid broke—not in a "throw a tantrum" way—but in a "make everything in a ten-mile radius scream" kind of way.

I remember standing at the edge of it all, feeling the pressure like I was inside a microwave built by gods who never read the manual. And in the middle of the chaos, Johnny just . . . breathed.

Then he walked into the flames. Turned around once. Said, "No more running."

I woke up clutching my chest. My heart wasn't racing, it was *mourning*. Like I'd lost something I never had.

I don't know who the kid was, but if I ever find him, I'd buy him a soda and tell him he's braver than I ever was.

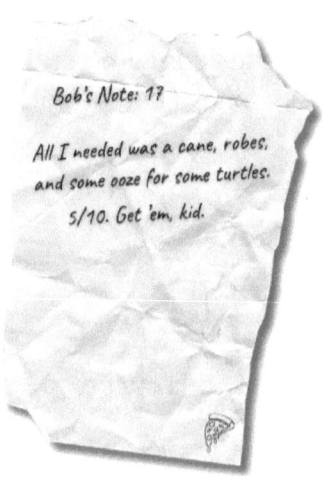

Bob's Note: 17

All I needed was a cane, robes, and some ooze for some turtles.

5/10. Get 'em, kid.

The Hall of Failed Faces

An infinite hallway, its walls lined with the ghosts of my failures—framed photographs of everyone I'd let down, disappointed, or inadvertently harmed.

Some wept silently, their sorrow a palpable presence. Some screamed with a sound I couldn't hear, their anguish trapped.

Others offered smiles, a terrible, quiet forgiveness that felt like a brand. They had seemingly released the Bob who wronged them.

But within me, the ledger of guilt remained open. Forgiveness was a currency I couldn't access, especially for myself.

Bob's Note: 18   God, I hate myself.

The Bud Gambit

It's night. Rain lashed down because the universe has a flair for pathetic fallacy when someone's about to catch a bullet.

The job: dust Bud Berkman, ex-cop turned PI, a creature fueled by black coffee and pure spite, looked like he'd crawl out of a building collapse just to file a noise complaint.

I had the high ground, rooftop sniper perch, clean shot—textbook execution.

Then I saw him.

Across the street, another rooftop. Me. Same hangdog face, same bargain-bin suit (different shade, though—that Bob had marginally better taste). And his rifle wasn't on Bud. It was locked on my forehead. We both went rigid. The realization slammed home. One Bob, the hitter. The other, apparently, Bud's ridiculously improbable guardian angel.

"Shit," I hissed into the downpour.

Across the way, my mirror image nodded, a grim acknowledgment. "Yup."

We fired as one—a blossoming inferno in my chest. My rifle slid away. Falling back, the cold rain mingled with my blood's sudden warmth.

My last glimpse was Bud Berkman, that charmed bastard, diving for cover and trading shots with a *third* crew of masked shooters trying to ventilate him. Guy fought like a badger that had already rage-quit life twice. Maybe that was the secret.

Then blackness. No grand revelation. No dying insight.

Just two Bobs efficiently erased each other, accidentally granting another poor bastard another day of misery.

Still debating if that's ironic tragedy or the closest I'll ever get to accidentally doing something vaguely decent.

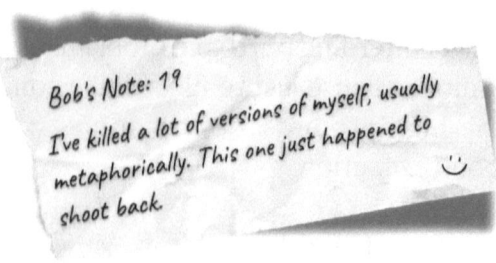

Bob's Note: 19
I've killed a lot of versions of myself, usually metaphorically. This one just happened to shoot back. ☺

God of Garbage Day

Power surged—I was a god.

I tried to make something good, something that mattered.

But everything I touched, every life I sparked, warped and curdled into another me. Only . . . amplified. The sadness was heavier, the anger sharper, more pathetic; my self-loathing multiplied.

In a moment of divine frustration, or rage, call it what you will—I drowned the whole damn mess. An ark? Didn't cross my mind.

Turns out being all-powerful is just another way to screw things up when you hate yourself this much.

Bob's Note: 20
4/10, I rather had sit with a damn magnifying glass tanning my taint.

The Door That Won't Open

There's this hallway I keep ending up in. Always the same.

Gray walls, flickering lights, buzzing overhead like something alive and dying at the same time. The kind of sterile, soul-sucking place where time doesn't move—just hangs there, sagging like the bags under your eyes after another sleepless night.

At the end of the hallway, there's a door. No handle. No knob. Just a fucking door, sitting there like a dare.

On the other side, I hear Jill's voice. She's crying. Not wailing. Not screaming. Just this quiet, hollow sob like she's been doing it for so long, there's no energy left for pain.

The kids are laughing—only it's distorted, like a cassette tape left on a dashboard in July. Twisted. Warped. Off.

I knock. I pound. I scream their names until my throat's raw and bloody. The door doesn't budge.

Behind me, I start to hear ticking. Not a clock. Something slower. Heavier. Like a countdown, but only meant for me. I turn around and nothing's there. Just the hallway stretching backward into a void I refuse to look too long at.

I keep trying the door. I beg. I curse. I claw at it like a goddamn animal.

Then I stop. I press my forehead to the cold surface. It feels like stone. It hums like it's alive.

I whisper, "Please."

Jill's crying stops.

So does the laughter.

And then . . . silence. Thick. Final.

I wake up with my heart trying to break out of my chest, my hands numb from how hard I've clenched them into fists.

And for a few seconds, I swear—I can still hear the ticking.

I don't know what's worse, that I can't open the door . . . or that I still think I might deserve to.

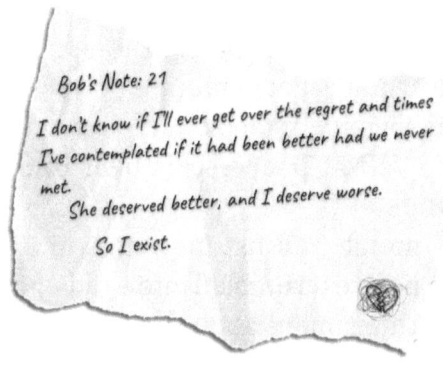

Bob's Note: 21

I don't know if I'll ever get over the regret and times I've contemplated if it had been better had we never met.
She deserved better, and I deserve worse.

So I exist.

Bear God of the Wastes

Consciousness returned in a desolate expanse. Stark post-fallout vibes: the endless sigh of sand, the skeletal remains of the past in rust, the phantom scent of radiation, and the heavy air of despair.

Then, the impossible. Blinking didn't help. Rubbing my eyes was pointless—a grizzly bear adorned in a suit of makeshift cybernetics. A mini nuclear fusion core pulsed on its back, and wore welding goggles perched like bizarre spectacles.

It spoke, its voice the sound of mountains crumbling into a canyon of coffee grounds, declaring itself 'Ursa Major, Shepherd of Scraps, Lord of Rust, and Guardian of the Lost.' We found solace on a shattered tank, sharing thoughts on being, nothingness, the art of improvised weaponry, the brutal ballet of mutant power struggles, and the undeniable divinity of tacos.

Strangely, I felt at peace. This bear understood the wasteland within.

A massive, metal-clad fist met mine in a surprisingly tender gesture before it rumbled into a radioactive haze, its voice fading with a lament about needing more industrial adhesive.

Pretty sure I just encountered something sacred, or at least a kindred spirit in a far more impressive package than my own reflection.

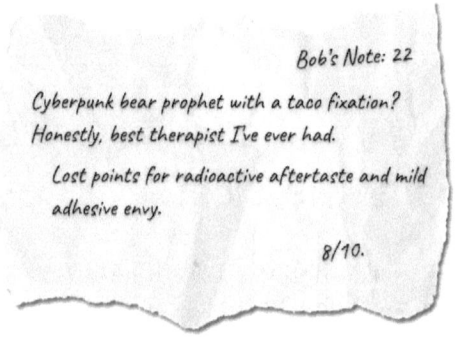

Bob's Note: 22

Cyberpunk bear prophet with a taco fixation? Honestly, best therapist I've ever had.

Lost points for radioactive aftertaste and mild adhesive envy.

8/10.

The Fox and the Fall

I was falling. That's it. Just falling.

Some tower. No clue why I was up there. Clock tower, maybe? Something *vaguely symbolic*. Time. Regret. Probably guilt. You get the idea.

The wind whipped my face like it had a vendetta. I tried screaming, but all that came out was a whimper and half a line from *Bohemian Rhapsody*.

Then I saw them.

At first, I thought it was a gargoyle. Perched up top, unmoving, theatrical as hell. Then it *moved*. And *shifted*. And *jumped*.

Wings. Huge. Feathers so red they glowed. Not fire—just *intent*.

The thing—no, *they*—swooped down, talons slicing the air, and caught me mid-fall like I was Frodo getting saved by one of Gandalf's Uber-eagles.

We soared upward, the city spinning below. I caught a glimpse of myself in a building's reflection—arms flailing, face pale, hair doing some anime-level wind physics.

They dropped me off on a rooftop with all the ceremony of a pizza delivery.

"Be more careful next time," they said, voice muffled through a kabuki mask.

Blood-red leather armor. Foxlike grace. They didn't just walk—they *glided*.

Before I could get a "thanks" out, they shifted again—into a goddamn fox—and leaped into the alley below, disappearing like it was routine.

I stood there for a good minute, waiting to wake up.

I didn't. At least not right away.

Just stood on that rooftop, wondering:

Who the hell was that?

Why did they feel familiar?

And why do I feel like I've met them before . . . or will again?

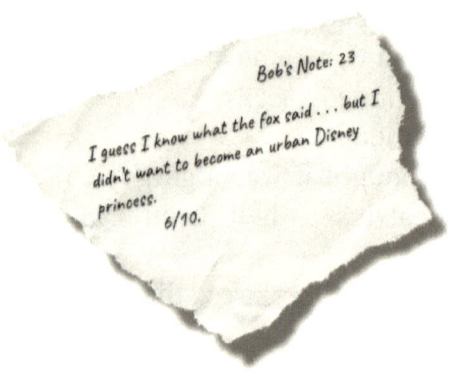

Bob's Note: 23

I guess I know what the fox said . . . but I didn't want to become an urban Disney princess.   6/10.

The Loop

I'm watching myself die. Again.

Not metaphorically, not in some fuzzy dream logic way. I'm *literally* standing there—off to the side, like a director on a terrible low-budget snuff film—watching versions of me meet their end in every way imaginable.

132

Hanging. Drowning. Burning. Shooting. Jumping off something tall and final. Eating myself into oblivion. Slipping on a banana peel straight into traffic—okay, that one was weirdly specific and tragically comedic.

Each one ends the same. Lights out. No applause.

But the weird part? After each death, *he—me—*turns and looks right at me. Like he *knows* I'm watching.

And smiles.

That kind of smile you give a friend who still doesn't get the joke. That "you poor bastard" grin that says, *you still think this ends differently, huh?*

One of them—maybe the fifth or fifteenth version, who knows—leans in real close to the invisible fourth wall and says, "We're all still here, Bob. You're the one that keeps leaving."

And then he blows his brains out.

The blood spells something on the wall behind him. I can't read it. Every time I blink, the letters rearrange themselves like a cruel game of Wheel of Misfortune.

I try to walk away, but I can't. My feet are stuck in something thick. Something that feels like guilt and smells like failure.

The screen goes dark. Another me appears. This one's in a hospital bed. He's flatlining. Nurses rush in, but they're all *me*, too.

The loop resets. Again. And again. And again.

Each Bob dies a little differently. But I'm always the one left watching, left wondering if this time—maybe this time—it'll stop.

It never does.

I wake up sweating through my sheets, heart galloping, throat dry.

Still here. Still stuck.

But hey, at least I'm the Bob who gets to write it down.

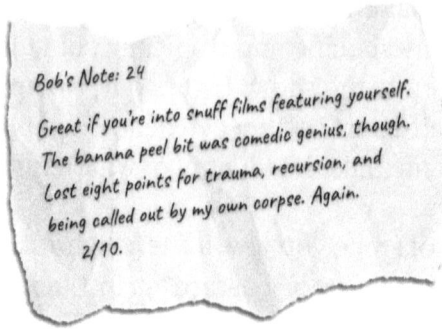

Bob's Note: 24

Great if you're into snuff films featuring yourself.
The banana peel bit was comedic genius, though.
Lost eight points for trauma, recursion, and
being called out by my own corpse. Again.
2/10.

They Can't Hear You in the Void

In the sterile confines of a hospital bed, I screamed into a void of my own making, my throat aching with unheard pleas. The world around me remained indifferent. Then, a nurse turned, her eyes holding the weight of ages, yet devoid of emotion.

But she saw beyond the physical—she saw *me*, unmoored above the failing flesh.

Her voice, a dry whisper from the edge of oblivion, confirmed my deepest fear: "You were never truly here, were you?"

The heart monitor's rhythmic pulse dissolved into a flat, unwavering line.

The fragile tether snapped.

And with it, the last semblance of my own reality.

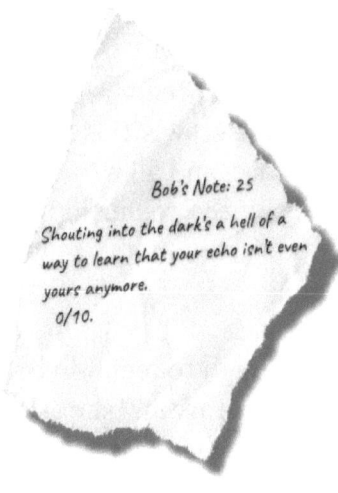

Bob's Note: 25

Shouting into the dark's a hell of a way to learn that your echo isn't even yours anymore.

0/10.

Butterfly in a Body Bag

I'm in a morgue. One of those industrial ones—metal walls, flickering lights, the smell of freezer burn and antiseptic death. Cold enough to freeze your regret right off.

There's a row of body bags laid out like a dinner buffet for Thanatos. All zipped. All silent.

Except one.

It twitches. Then again. A sharp, shivering jolt like something waking up mid-autopsy. The bag starts to inflate and pulse—slow at first, then violent, like something inside *wants out.*

The zipper unzips itself. Yeah. All the way down, like a magician's flourish. Out crawls this *thing*—part woman, part moth, part nightmare, and all wrong.

Wings so wide they hit the ceiling lights. Eyes that glow like dying stars. Her body shimmers like wet velvet, but it's the voice that gets me.

I *know* it.

Not entirely. Just enough to feel it in my teeth.

"Would you die for them again?" she asks. Her voice isn't loud—it's gentle. Like silk against a blade.

I try to answer. I *want* to say yes, or no, or anything at all.

But I can't. My jaw doesn't work. My mouth is full of thick, rubbery pressure. I reach up, and my tongue is *gone.* Melted? Swallowed? I don't know. It's just . . . not there anymore.

And she just keeps *watching.* No judgment. Just waiting.

The wings start to fold around me, cocoon-like. I can feel the dust in my lungs and taste it in my throat, like old parchment and funeral flowers.

And then I understand.

She wasn't asking if I'd *die* for them.

She was asking if I'd do *it* again.

And again. And again. And again.

The bag zips closed over us both.

I wake up coughing, mouth dry, the taste of ashes and silence lingering like a prayer I never finished.

Bob's Note: 26

I think I may have developed some new weird fetish. No clue.
7/10.

The Red Right Hand

I'm strapped to this dinner chair like it's my fucking throne—chains cold, tight, and familiar, like I've worn them longer than I've worn my own skin.

The table's set for six. All the plates are bleeding.

Not metaphorically. I mean *actually bleeding*—thick, red, slow like molasses. Dripping over the edge, soaking into the linen, pooling under mashed potatoes and roast beef like dinner's been served straight from a butcher's back alley nightmare.

And then it shows up.

A severed red right hand—gloved, crawling across the table like a goddamn spider on Sunday best. Doesn't scuttle. It *struts*. One finger taps a glass of wine, another flicks a dinner roll off the edge. Real classy, this one.

It stops in front of me.

I try to look away, but I can't move my head. Can't even blink. Then the voice comes from behind. Smooth. Too close. Like it's breathing down my neck but never touching.

"Not yet," it says. "You're not done cooking."

Cooking what?

Then the hand points at my chest.

I look down.

There's a hole in me. Not a metaphorical hole. Not the spiritual kind your therapist tells you is "normal after loss." This is literal. Empty. Carved clean. Hollowed out like a jack-o'-lantern that forgot Halloween ended months ago.

And the worst part?

I'm *warm* inside.

Like the oven's still on. Like whatever I'm supposed to become isn't ready yet.

I try to scream, but the chain tightens across my throat, and the hand pats my cheek—gentle, approving. Like I'm doing a good job becoming whatever the hell I'm meant to be.

Then I wake up.

Chest aching. Breath ragged. Still feeling hollow.

Still cooking.

What do the kids say nowadays? 'I guess we're cooked now, chat.' Whatever.

Bob's Note: 27

3/10. Needs more Halloween!

Welcome to Bob's World

A city stretching into an impossible distance, populated solely by reflections of myself.

Infinite Bobs, each a different age, wearing the ghosts of past and imagined lives, but all carrying the same heavy burden of inadequacy in their gaze. This was a universe sculpted from my own shortcomings.

One version—older, cloaked in a ridiculously worn trench coat—approached, his nod a grim acknowledgment.

"We've been waiting," he said, his voice echoing with the weight of countless disappointments.

Then the laughter began, a booming, horrific symphony of self-rejection that filled the desolate cityscape.

And the terrifying truth?

I was part of it, the laughter bubbling up from within, unstoppable.

I woke up, the echo of that laughter still clinging to me, a cold premonition settling in. This was a bad sign.

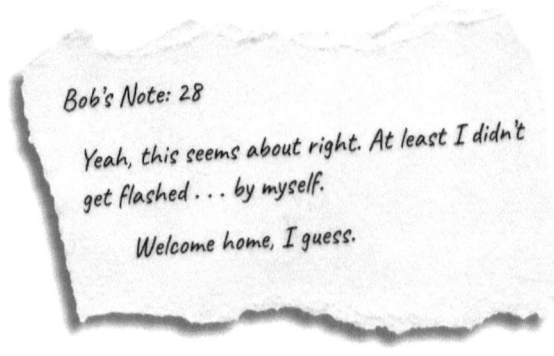

Bob's Note: 28

Yeah, this seems about right. At least I didn't get flashed . . . by myself.

Welcome home, I guess.

The Nano War of the Future, Past, Present

The tech was all sleek chrome and pulsing lights. The plot? Pure Cronenberg. I'm pretty sure the government had either imploded or achieved total mind control. The distinction felt increasingly academic.

Nanomachines powered everything and everyone. These were not just handy gadgets—microscopic robots rewrote thoughts and puppeteered flesh. The world was a seamless, sterile nightmare designed by . . . well . . . any tech giant's evil twin.

Somehow, I'd stumbled into a motley crew of rebels lurking in the system's glitches—paranoid ex-scientists, twitchy soldiers haunted by code, and assorted beautiful losers. A kid was like part white tiger. One guy spoke solely in mangled Bon Jovi. A woman briefly clipped through reality when she sneezed.

We were, naturally, humanity's last desperate gamble, armed with stolen algorithms and a healthy dose of existential dread.

I found myself sporting a trench coat (apparently standard issue for temporal screw-ups), dual EMP pistols, and absolutely no idea what the hell I was doing. But it felt . . . right. Like a broken piece of me finally clicked into place, fighting the digital ghost in the machine.

We stormed some kind of central processing nexus. Alarms blared, explosions rocked the sterile corridors, and data screamed in binary. I'm pretty sure I bought it, taking out the core. I felt myself unraveling into lines of code.

Woke up feeling . . . strangely conductive. Like my fillings had staged a hostile takeover.

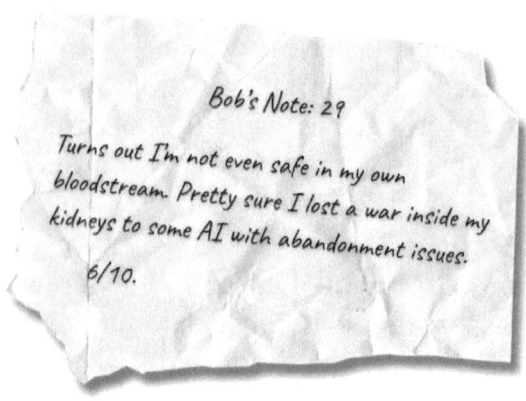

Bob's Note: 29

Turns out I'm not even safe in my own bloodstream. Pretty sure I lost a war inside my kidneys to some AI with abandonment issues.

6/10.

The Devil Wears Red (Right) Hands

He was back—the older man with the unsettlingly red right hand. This time, he sat across from me in a diner that offered no sustenance but only choices, the unnatural smoothness of his gloved hand catching the dim light.

He leaned in, his voice a low, persuasive murmur, offering a deal etched in shadow.

One innocent life traded for peace. "No more pain, Bob," he'd said, his smile unwavering. "Just one life. Yours to take."

I laughed, a hollow, brittle sound. I called him a cosmic used car salesman peddling damnation. He just smiled, a knowing, patient expression.

I woke up clutching a fork, its tines sharp against my palm, feeling like a makeshift dagger.

No appetite for breakfast today.

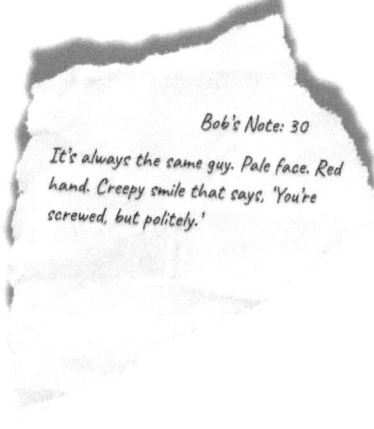

Bob's Note: 30

It's always the same guy. Pale face. Red hand. Creepy smile that says, 'You're screwed, but politely.'

Multiversal Glimpses of Me, Myself, and Fucked

I saw them—a dizzying kaleidoscope of me. Happy Bobs. Shattered Bobs. Bobs with receding hairlines. One even had a goddamn cat. Another was President (that one's eyes held a chilling, vacant power).

Some were bathed in love. Others were monstrous.

One stared directly through the fractured realities, his gaze locking with mine, and whispered, "We're all you."

I screamed awake, my hands clawing at my face, a desperate attempt to erase the image. I couldn't remember what that one looked like.

But I knew, with a chilling certainty, it was me.

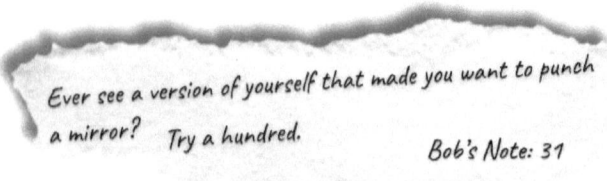

Ever see a version of yourself that made you want to punch a mirror? Try a hundred.

Bob's Note: 31

A Nightmare in Reverse

No screams tore through the quiet. No grotesque visions danced in the dark. No sudden explosions shattered the stillness. Just... absolute silence, a heavy weight pressing down on my chest.

I walked through a dream devoid of sound. My footsteps made no echo. I tried to speak, but my voice was trapped, a silent scream in my throat.

It was calm, yes. But not the comforting kind. The kind that smelled faintly of formaldehyde and felt like unseen eyes watching from beneath the floorboards.

When I woke up, I actually missed the screaming.

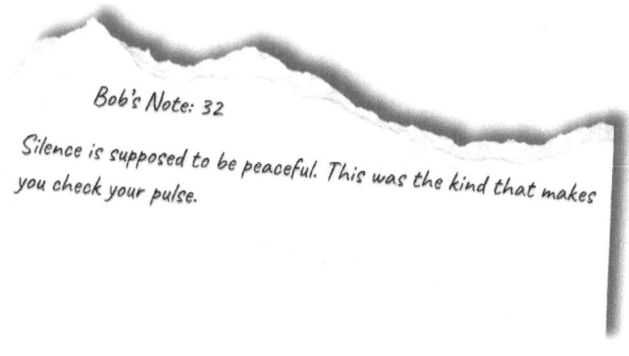

Bob's Note: 32

Silence is supposed to be peaceful. This was the kind that makes you check your pulse.

A Feather

A single black feather drifted down from a sky I couldn't even see.

Landed in my outstretched hand like it had been waiting for me all along.

Warm. Soft. Humming with a faint vibration that made zero goddamn sense in the usual chaos of my brain.

Nothing in my life ever felt peaceful. Nothing ever stayed.

But this?

It didn't burn. Didn't dissolve. Didn't turn into a knife or middle finger like so many of my dream props tend to do.

It just *was*—resting in my palm, like it belonged.

I swear I heard a crow . . . or maybe a raven.

No words. No warning. Just that feather and the sound of wings on the edge of sleep.

When I woke up, my hand was empty.

But for once, something in me felt . . . lighter.

I caught a feather. Didn't even sneeze. Bob's Note: 33
That's how I knew it wasn't real.

Jill's Note

It starts with footsteps. Mine, I think.

They echo through a house that *used* to be mine. Except it isn't, not really. It's too long. Too narrow. Every door I pass is slightly open, just enough to see shadows writhing behind them—like memories that don't want to be remembered.

The walls are gray, sterile. No pictures. No furniture. Just that awful smell of dust and something . . . burnt.

Then I see it—my wallet, lying open on a hallway table that shouldn't exist. There's a note sticking out of it. Bright red. Practically glowing in this drab-ass dreamscape. I reached for it, and I already knew it was from Jill.

It's her handwriting. No mistaking it. That little loopy 'y' at the end of *you*, the way she underlines too hard and presses the pen like she's trying to carve her thoughts into time itself.

But the words . . .

They won't stay still.

"We love you," it says.

Then, "You failed us."

"Wakeup."

"It wasn't your fault."

"It was always your fault."

Then, just a "?"

I blink, and the note flickers like an old film reel spitting smoke. The words warp, twist, and rearrange. They start bleeding, literally dripping crimson ink—or blood—onto my fingers.

I hold it tighter, desperate to lock it into something real, something stable. I try to fold it, to save it.

That's when it catches fire.

No spark. No sound. Just . . . *foomph*—and it's gone. Like it never mattered.

And then I hear her voice. Not behind me. *Inside* me.

Soft. Sad. Almost tired.

"Do you really think you'd still be here if I hated you?"

I try to turn. I want to see her. Just once. But there's only the hallway again. Empty. Longer.

So much longer now.

I woke up crying, not from fear.

From *hope*.

Fuck.

The Booth

Grave's Diner. Or maybe the flickering neon sign read 'Limbo Lounge'?

I slid into a booth opposite two grim-faced individuals named Dana and Walter. They were deep in conversation—recent homicides, some giant terrorizing fast-food chains, a spate of witch or demonic activity—the usual Monday morning digest.

I sat beside them, drawn by an odd compulsion. "Hello, boys. Been waiting long?"

They just nodded, like weary travelers between dimensions, my intrusion barely registering.

I ordered the cherry pie that had the shape of a heart in a poker suit on it. When I cut into it, a thick, dark blood oozed onto the plate.

I ate it anyway.

I didn't ask questions as it seemed the wisest course of action.

Felt like I crashed someone else's bizarre Monday morning meeting.   Bob's Note: 35

Dragons and Diapers

Open eyes. Blink. World gone wild. Towering trees. Razor-sharp mountains against a sky that looked digitally enhanced. Air thick with pine, wet dirt, and a primal, untamed scent.

Then, holy shit, dragons. Lots of them. Big, scaly bastards, roaring like the end of days, and spitting actual fire. Everywhere.

My survival strategy? Run like hell.

Immediate fail: tripped over a fern older than my therapist.

Immediate consequence: total pants malfunction (apparently, fear is a universal language my bladder speaks fluently).

Played dead, praying dragons weren't into heavily soiled snacks.

Nope. One landed right next to me, its shadow a suffocating blanket. Its eye, ancient and way too knowing, fixed on mine.

And then . . . a wink. A giant, scaly, *are-you-kidding-me?* wink. Before it roared back into the sky to rejoin its fire-breathing buddies.

The rest is a blur of shame and a lingering . . . aroma. But yeah, the view was pretty spectacular.

For about five seconds.

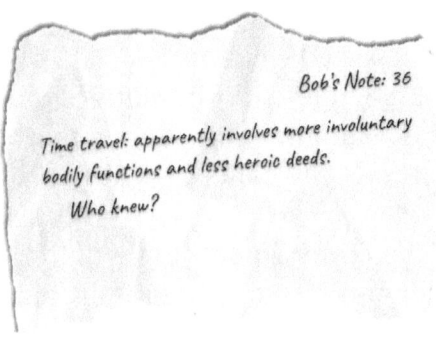

Bob's Note: 36

Time travel: apparently involves more involuntary bodily functions and less heroic deeds.

Who knew?

Reluctant Chaperone to the Dead

Standing in a fog-choked field, the grayness swallowed all sound. Limbo felt . . . plausible.

A small gathering of children stood nearby, their forms barely there, their fear a palpable weight in the silence. Clearly untethered.

One boy, his eyes a hauntingly familiar echo—a cop's lost son from a forgotten thread of time—pointed, his voice a breath in the stillness. "It's you," he whispered. "The one who treads where life and death blur. The Walker Between Worlds."

Wonderful. Just wonderful.

Apparently, I was their guide. My burden: to lead these fragile souls across the misty expanse to . . . the unknown destination of departed children.

And, of course, the shadows came. Slithering horrors born of the fog. Hungry voids, things that craved what remained of their innocence, creatures of teeth and endless need.

I fought, fueled by something I didn't understand. A blade of shimmering grief and guilt materialized—a surprisingly potent weapon.

Did I deliver them? Did I escape the fog myself?

The memory dissolved, the little boy's spectral hand finding a moment of solidity in mine. "Thank you, Mister Bob," he whispered, a weightless blessing.

I woke up feeling like I'd carried a universe of sorrow, my body aching with phantom burdens.

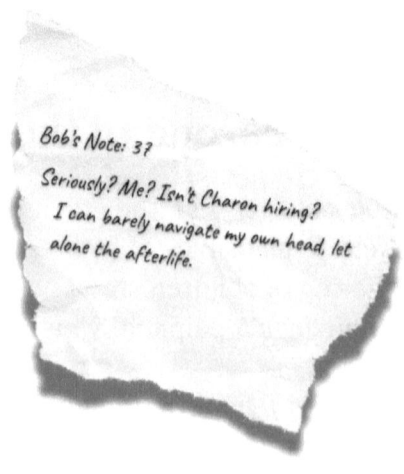

Bob's Note: 3?

Seriously? Me? Isn't Charon hiring? I can barely navigate my own head, let alone the afterlife.

Flame, Fight, Flicker

Something had shifted in the deep, shadowed corners of my mind.

The air in the room felt less stagnant, less heavy—a subtle lightening I hadn't noticed in a long time.

I'd dreamt of standing at a crossroads, but not one that led to the familiar abyss of death. Just . . . life. Messy. Stupid. Loud. Unfair.

And, somehow, I chose to walk forward.

No monsters clawed at the edges of my vision. No Man with the Red Right Hand offered insidious deals. No ghostly family mourned my absence.

Just me, on a cracked and broken road, drawing a shaky breath that tasted of stale air, a reminder of the darkness I was leaving behind.

I woke up and didn't scream, cry, or even flinch. I just stared at the ceiling, a fragile thought forming: "Okay. Let's try again."

That had to be progress. Right?

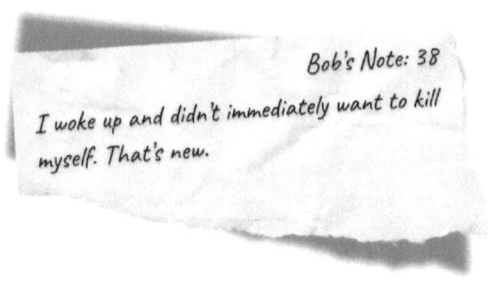

Bob's Note: 38
I woke up and didn't immediately want to kill myself. That's new.

Moments of Sunshine

That slight darkness—the one where you know your eyes are closed, and yep, there's the sun. I opened mine and instantly knew where I was.

The sky was so blue you'd swear it was the ocean. Planes cut through the azure like lazy sharks above. The grass beneath me? Soft. Plush. Like a bed made of all the naps I never got to take. Cicadas played their summer song, dogs barked somewhere nearby, and my kids and wife were in my arms. Hell, I didn't want to get up.

I kissed each of their foreheads.

Over there. I hear them. That's. . . Dad. Mom.

I sat up and looked toward the picnic tables.

It's our summer bash. Our tradition. Grandma. Grandpa. Everyone's here. Even the in-laws on my wife's side—*and nobody's fighting.*

Burgers and hot dogs on the grill, corn, wedges, coleslaw, mom's potato and macaroni salad, a cobbler, pie—all of it. The scent of charcoal pulled me back to grilling with Pops and sneaking bites of burger patties, laughing like we were sharing a secret with the smoke.

Laughter. Conversation. Love.

This is peace.

There's no fighting. No passive-aggressive jabs. No one is missing. No drunk slurs or arguments over politics. No itch in the back of my skull. No gnawing thought telling me something's wrong with me.

But I know. *Fuck,* do I know.

It's been years. Ages. Some of you aren't even alive anymore. Some of you don't speak to me. Some of you . . . You left when I needed you most, or I was guided in another direction.

Still . . . this? This is nice.

I want to live in this lie forever.

But it's getting darker.

No. Please. *Please don't go.*

Mom. Dad. Everyone.

Just one more minute. Let me have this one fucking moment that feels *good.*

Please. Don't take it away from me.

I know it's not real. I *know.*

I KNOW.

JUST ONE MORE MINUTE!

LET ME TELL THEM!

LET ME TELL ALL OF THEM!

I wake up.

Tears already sliding down my face. I'm cold. Too cold.
And I cry.
And I cry.
Until I fall asleep again, hoping, praying for a rerun.
Hoping that maybe, this time, I can tell you:
I *love you.*
I *miss you.*

Just Like a Mirror

"Hey. I'm talking to you."

My reflection in the mirror didn't just look back; it *reached out* from the glass, its gaze locking onto mine, pulling me in. Mean. Spiteful. Disappointed. "Nah, don't look away like you don't hear me, bud, because I know damn well you can fucking hear me. Look at me when I am talking to you—look me in the eyes."

The reflection's lips moved, twisting into a sneer. "Do you think you can mope around because you're having an 'off day?' Can't you see that there's shit that needs to be done?"

Another excuse formed on my lips, but the reflection's voice cut through it like glass shards. "Nah, don't give me that shit."

Its gaze hardened, pinning me like an accusing finger. My own eyes fell, heavy with shame, guilt, and regret.

"We're not the only ones that have shit going on, OK?" The reflection softened, a brief crack in the hostility.

"There's shit to do, cleaning to be done, jobs to hunt, therapy to go to. Alright? Your wife's getting real fucking tired of your 'Woe is me' bullshit. Set an example for your kids. Get your shit together."

I mumbled something incoherent, the sound lost between us.

The reflection *slapped* me with its fury, a jolt deeper than skin. "Excuse me? Nah, don't play that put-off shit game with me. I know you. I am you. Remember, fuck nuts? The shit that's happened in the past is in the past. We can't change that."

A sigh passed over my reflection's face, weary and defeated. "Look. I am sorry. I snapped. It's just . . . I get it. Things are tough. Our thoughts—my head—our head is fucked up. Yeah, I know we had a pretty good breakthrough in therapy, did that whole EMDR shit and spilled our fucking hearts out, and almost . . . almost let the cat out of the bag, but hey, we're gonna be fine. Alright?"

I looked back, the words catching in my throat. The reflection's eyes widened in genuine shock. "What? What do you mean by saying that you want to quit? You—you can't, man." The voice echoing from the glass turned threatening. "If you do, we'll probably throw away all the fucking progress we've made!"

"Woah, woah, calm down—remember, your temper will get you in trouble, bud." I heard myself say, a desperate attempt to quell the storm in the glass.

But the reflection didn't calm down. It seethed, a maelstrom of anger, resentment, regret, and hate. The glass groaned, then shattered, mirroring the breaking point.

"Great. Just. Fucking. Great."

I stared at the splintered pieces of myself, at the shards reflecting fragmented fury and shame. "You know you're gonna have to cover this up? Or are you gonna tell Carol about it and risk getting fucking admitted? Fuck off, man, C'MON!"

My eyes scanned the broken mess. "I said I am done being tied to my past, to the things I said, that I did, and being chained to whatever bullshit fate that I was predisposed to." My voice dropped, firm. "I am not them. I am not that person anymore. I will be the phoenix that rises and burns it all to the ground!"

With swift, decisive movements, the broken pieces were swept into the garbage pail, then the dumpster.

An echo reached my ears.

A phantom pain.

Dad.

"You've come a long way, kid. I'm proud of you. I just thought I'd tell you that."

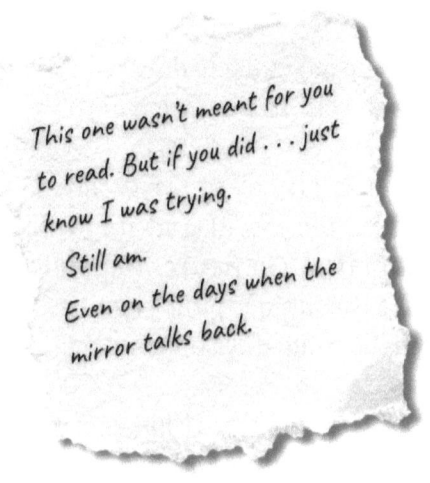

This one wasn't meant for you to read. But if you did . . . just know I was trying.

Still am.

Even on the days when the mirror talks back.

In the End

Bob looked down at the battered and old notebook on the table beside the beat-up hospital bed. Like him, the yellow had almost faded and had seen better days. He flipped it open to the next blank page and let out a short, harsh laugh. With a stolen hospital pen, he wrote:

> *Starting a new gig in a few days. I'll die, but I can still say "fuck you" to the cancer.*□

> *In other news, I'll get to write shit down for the universe—the world and its problems—in addition to mine. Go figure. Hopefully, it'll be decent, and I won't get paid peanuts. Hell, who knows, maybe some day someone will read it?* □

> *Eh, it's getting to feel like everyone else's problems keep bleeding and melding with mine anyway. Well, imaginary reader... wish me luck. Maybe I'll be balls deep in your reality next.*

He let a smirk escape as he closed it and tossed it back on the table.

Then, he looked out the window and sighed. "I'm getting too old for this whole every day is an existential crisis bullshit."

THE END FOR NOW . . .
BOB WILL RETURN

ACKNOWLEDGEMENTS

Thanks to my friends and family for your continued support.

Thanks to the Vapors of Morphine, Morphine, Buckethead, Interpol, and (even more) countless others for fueling me with countless hours of great music on my projects.

As I sought to revise this and other projects, I want to thank the following bands: Ghost, Priest, Magna Carta Cartel, Avatar, Volbeat, Gojira, Gothminister, and Night Club. Seriously, I love you all.

Robin Williams, for all the laughs and for showing that even those with happy faces are sad on the inside.

Chester Bennington, thank you for all the music you created and for helping me get through some of the most challenging times of my life.

My friends and family, and others that have either attempted or committed suicide.

My *World of Warcraft* friends on the US server Aegwynn and those in the Horde guild, Revolt. You're all demoted to "Used Tissue." RIP Bork and Zalash.

With love,

Sin

Lastly, to you, my lovely readers. Anyone else I may have forgotten to mention . . . thank you.

ABOUT THE AUTHOR

Robert J. McCartney is the author behind *This is Bob* and the ongoing **Willborne Saga**, which includes *Requiem for Lilith* and *Lilah's Guide to Hoyle*. He writes strange and human stories that explore identity, autonomy, and the will to defy fate—often wrapped in dark humor, dream logic, or emotional gut punches.

He lives in Tennessee with his wife, their two children, and an ever-growing backlog of games. When he's not writing or working under his independent label, A.B.Normal Publishing and Media Group, he's probably logged into *World of Warcraft* or plotting the next chapter in his ever-expanding universe.

This is Bob was initially released as *The Chronicles of Bob: The Chronic Suicidal*, a fictional lens for confronting mental illness, trauma, and grief.

He also writes an ongoing web series called *The Diary of the Wasteland Bear God*. To read more about Robert's worlds—or to reach out—visit www.abnormalpublishing.com.

For You

I was thinking . . .

What would be nice—no, what's something that'd be nice to share with folks without needing to overly stuff in this thing?

Music.

It helps—it's something we can all (more or less) find common ground on. Sure, we all have our tastes, but that's just being human, right? Well, I figured, why not make a little something for folks; give them an earful—create a soundtrack to the noise that's bumpin' around in my old noggin.

So, I did, not for me but for you.

I mean, I have my playlist. And the other Bob, well, he's got his, and trust me, he's got plenty. At times, it may as well be "same shit, just put it on repeat and shuffle," but it's fine. It's good. Because sometimes, keeping that safety net that you've made from memories, thoughts (the good, the bad, and ugly), and sounds that give . . . take . . . and help fuel your treading into the next day are all that you need.

So, take it if you will. Is it perfect? Nah. Like me, you, and anyone and everyone else in the world, in existence and beyond. There's room for improvement.

If you like what you hear or want something more, drop me a line at https://www.abnormalpublishing.com/contact-us.

When it comes to music, it's great to hear others' thoughts, suggestions, and recommendations.

Adios.

With love,

Bob Barnem

;

Scan this QR code for a Spotify playlist: This is Bob: A Playlist to Not Dying (Mostly)

*Scan this QR code for
a Spotify playlist: The
Man with the Red Right
Hand*